PROTECTING OLIVIA

SPECIAL FORCES: OPERATION ALPHA

RILEY EDWARDS

Dear Readers,

Welcome to the Special Forces: Operation Alpha Fan-Fiction world!

If you are new to this amazing world, in a nutshell the author wrote a story using one or more of my characters in it. Sometimes that character has a major role in the story, and other times they are only mentioned briefly. This is perfectly legal and allowable because they are going through Aces Press to publish the story.

This book is entirely the work of the author who wrote it. While I might have assisted with brainstorming and other ideas about which of my characters to use, I didn't have any part in the process or writing or editing the story.

I'm proud and excited that so many authors loved my characters enough that they wanted to write them into their own story. Thank you for supporting them, and me!

READ ON!

Xoxo

Susan Stoker

BEFORE YOU BEGIN

Thank you for purchasing Protecting Olivia. I'm beyond thrilled to write in Susan Stoker's Special Forces: Operation Alpha universe. I've been a fan of Susan's for many years and have read every book she's published (multiple times.) While I've tried my hardest to stay true to her original characters (because, *hello*, they are already awesome) I am not Susan, I wrote them as I, the reader, experienced them. I want fans of the SOP series to feel like they're visiting old friends when they see, Tex, Wolf, Abe, and Caroline. I hope that I did her beloved characters justice. But please remember, I've taken some liberties.

I hope you enjoy the world I've created for you as much as I loved writing it.

To Extortion 17

The world lost 31 Heroes 06 Aug 2011. SOC SEAL John W. Faas was among the crew that died that day. Even in death, John continues to inspire all those who knew him and love him. He is not forgotten - never forgotten. His sacrifice and that of his family's reminds us that freedom is never free. We sleep soundly in our beds because rough men stand ready in the night to visit violence on those who would do us harm.

PROLOGUE

"Are you sure?" Timothy Clark asked Violet Myers one more time.

"A hundred percent. The call logs initiated from the prison have been erased. I double checked," Violet huffed.

She wasn't an idiot. Not by a long shot. She'd worked at the FBI's BAU for six years before she'd gone to the CIA where her propensity for information gathering and behavior analysis was put to better use. That was why'd she'd been chosen. That and she was weak. Too bad for her she wasn't smart enough to get herself out of her current situation.

"Good," Timothy spoke into the cellphone speaker in his hand before turning to me. "Everything is ready," he unnecessarily told me, as if I couldn't hear Violet over the speaker.

"Outstanding. May I?" I motioned for him to hand me the phone.

He easily obeyed handing me the phone. Timothy Clark was a fool and had no sense of self-preservation. His usefulness had run out, and just like anything else that was no longer valuable, it was time to dispose of him. Setting the phone on the table careful not to disconnect the call, I pulled my Browning M1911 from the holster and raised it level with Timothy's head.

The shot rang out in the room, and I relished the ringing in my ears. It reminded me of my days in the Army. When I had sworn allegiance to Bolivia, until my county had turned her back on me. And I found someone who could appreciate my abilities. Why had I been trained to kill, if not to kill?

"Oh, God. What was that?" Violet asked.

"Plans have changed, Ms. Meyers. You will be dealing with me directly from now on," I informed her.

"Where's Timothy?" she asked.

Stupid woman. Why did people always feel the need to ask questions when they already knew the answers?

"Gone. I'll be in touch soon." Before she could inquire any further I disconnected and pocketed Timothy's phone.

"Clean this up," I yelled to Juan. "Wrap him in plastic and shove him in the wall." I laughed at the thought of the girl sitting in a room with a rotting corpse in the wall. "Drywall the rest of the wall and use the extra wallpaper to finish it off."

I chose this house because it was secluded and had been foreclosed on. The bank had turned the utilities on now that it had been placed on the market. It was perfect for what I needed. It looked like the previous owners had been in the middle of renovations. Three of the four walls had been wallpapered, but the forth had been stripped down to the studs. It could've been a beautiful home; too bad it wouldn't be standing when I was done with it.

"Carlo?" I yelled to one of my men. "Are you ready? It's time to get the girl and bring her home."

1

LEO

Jesus H. Christ. I was going to kill my sister. She was always getting into some kind of crazy shit. She blamed her friends for the trouble they got themselves into, but I knew her ass was the ringleader. When Arabella crooked her finger, people ran – they always had. The older she became, the worse it got. Now at twenty-one, her ass was out of control.

My ma needed to hurry up and marry her off so someone else could drag their ass out of bed at midnight to bail her out of jail. Tonight's bond was for trespassing and destruction of property. Pretty tame night for Bella. Her brand-new Jeep Wrangler was in police impound covered in mud after she and the lame brain pack, or *Giamope* as Ma likes to call them, decided to go mudding on private property. Her little ass was lucky I knew the desk sergeant, and he processed her paperwork fast. Another five minutes and I would've left her there to spend the night. I was exhausted and just wanted to get into bed.

My phone vibrated in my pocket, and I ignored it without even pulling it out. I did not want to listen to Ma tell me how she named her only daughter Arabella because it meant answered prayers, and after three boys, Ma thought that her prayers had indeed been answered when she had finally had a girl. Only now, Ma believed she should've named Arabella the devil. She was not wrong in that assessment. I adored my little sister, but she was a menace. We did this little song and dance every time Arabella was arrested.

The phone vibrated again, and against my better judgment, I pulled it out and looked at the caller ID. Fuck me, Garrett in the office at two in the morning was worse than Ma calling me to complain about her choice of names.

I slid my finger across the screen to unlock my phone and entered my security code.

"Yo."

"Sorry to call in the middle of the night, but Tex called. He was poking around and came across some information. Looks like your case just broke wide open. Shit's about to go nuclear. Meetup is at the barn house. I'm calling in Z," Garrett rushed out.

I liked Garrett. He was no-nonsense, straight to the point. He could bullshit with the best of them but knew when it was time to cut the shit and work. Now was one of those times.

For the past three weeks, we'd been trying to track down Olivia Cox, the only daughter of Pamela Cox. Pam was the First Lady's White House aide and best friend. This was not the type of operation that Z Corps would usually take. More than that, this type of case was not usually assigned to the company's best-trained operatives. The Red Team was typically reserved for high-priority Ops; top secret missions that required our unique skill set. A missing person case shouldn't have been assigned to us. But when the POTUS asked Zane for a favor, he couldn't turn him down. I was beginning to think the spoiled twenty-five-year-old party girl went on a bender and was in Las Vegas living it up. But her mother was worried sick, and that meant the First Lady, Clarissa Anderson, was worried, too. If Mrs. Anderson was worried, the President would fix it so his wife would rest easy.

Well shit, so much for sleep. I was so close my keys were already in the front door, yet I was so damn far away from my bed. "Copy that, I'll be there in ten," I responded.

The line went dead, and I pocketed my phone, pulled my keys from the lock, and headed back to my truck.

The drive through downtown Annapolis was easy this time of night. There was no traffic around the

Capitol building or any midshipmen wandering the streets happy to be off the Naval Academy grounds, even if only for a few minutes of freedom. Once I was out of the narrow streets of downtown Annapolis, I gunned the engine, enjoying the loud rumble of my newly installed exhaust. I hoped like hell we'd be stateside long enough for me to enjoy a few road trips.

Zane had a safe house located on the South River. It was a rundown barn on a five-acre lot. What made this particular barn unique was the basement. It was more of a fallout shelter than a basement, actually. It was fully kitted out with an armory, bunks, food, and water supply. We could easily hide someone there if necessary. We also had secure comms in and out of the bunker.

I pulled up to the building noting Z and Garrett were already there. Z's Rover and Garrett's GSX R750 motorcycle were parked next to a black sedan and a Porsche Panamera both with Washington DC plates. Christ Almighty, it was never a good sign when someone from DC paid us a visit.

I hurried and parked, anxious to find out why the hell it was so important to meet at two in the fucking morning. Yeah, I was tired and cranky. Making my way to the exterior door of the barn, I placed four fingers on the biometric scanner discretely placed under what looked to be a realtor's lockbox and impatiently waited for it to accept my fingerprints. The lock slid open, allowing me access to the interior of a dusty old barn; it was complete with straw bales, horse stalls, and the earthy musk smell one would expect. I didn't bother turning on the overhead light since I'd been here a hundred times and knew where the door was to the basement.

I fought back a sneeze and entered my eight-digit code, not that it mattered if I made noise. Whoever was in the basement already knew I was on the premises. There were perimeter alarms that had alerted them to my presence the moment I drove onto the property.

I opened the basement door, and my footsteps echoed as I rushed down the stairs and stopped at the final door. Placing my face inches away from the retinal scanner, I silently cursed Z. He was an over-the-top son-of-a-bitch when it came to the security. No one gained entrance to the inner sanctum of any company building uninvited.

All eyes snapped in my direction when I walked into the room. Any thought I had of sleep in the near future was shot to hell.

"Panther. Good to see you, son." A brisk voice called out from the crowd of people.

"Mr. President. Nice to see you as well, sir," I replied.

I quickly scanned the room, noting the President only had a two-man personal security detail, Gerald and Aaron, and no other secret service agents. He had a bad habit of sneaking off White House grounds, only taking his personal guards. I believe the last time the Secret Service agent in charge tried to talk to him about it, the President kindly reminded him of his years as a special operator and his time in the CIA. There might've been some expletives used on the President's end telling the agent where he could shove an inanimate object if he didn't like it. He was one tough old man.

Peter Newton stood off to the side looking disheveled and out of place in his pressed blue jeans and polo shirt. I had never seen the Attorney General in anything other than high-dollar designer suits.

It was still hard to believe that my boss, Zane, and Tom Anderson, the President of the United States, were close friends. I had known Zane a long time, and it wasn't until recently I found out just how deep his ties were to the President.

Our last mission was educational. Closely guarded secrets about a failed Russian op that resulted in the capture and torture of Jasmin Parker and Zane were brought to light. The torture Jasmin endured led to her losing her memory. I didn't know if I felt relief I could finally stop lying to Jasmin about her past, or if I was pissed as hell that Zane and Lincoln had kept their own secrets. Not a single person on our team knew that Zane had a brother. We certainly didn't know that Lincoln Parker, better known as Ghost, was that brother. We also didn't know that the President was Jasmin's uncle. One could say that the last month had been informative.

"Leo. Glad you're here," Zane said from his place across the room.

"Transport en route?" the President asked Gerald.

"Yes, sir. ETA two minutes," he answered.

"Great, let's go up," the President instructed.

Wordlessly the President's detail went for the door, Garrett followed with two desert tan Blackhawk messenger bags over his shoulder. I knew he had no less than four laptops and a tablet shoved in those bags. He gave the words computer geek a whole new meaning.

Zane trailed the President and the Attorney General, stopping at the door he turned to me. "You good?" he asked.

"Five by five," I answered. "Where are we going?"

"Tex's place."

"In Pennsylvania?" I inquired. I had never known Tex to invite anyone to his home.

"Roger."

"Who called in Tex?" I asked.

"He called us. He found something that requires a face-to-face. He requested the AG. Tom called and said he would be accompanying us."

"Well, hell. That cannot be good. Garrett said Tex had intel on the Cox case," I informed him. "One more thing. How did Tom know the AG was coming in?"

"Now that is the million-dollar question. I hate going in blind. Hopefully, Garrett will have something before we get to Pennsylvania. But if Tex wants a sit-down, shit has gone sideways. Everyone knows he prefers to conduct business via the dark web or phone. Hell, I've only met the guy once in person, and that was only because his man Wolf needed some intel from me. What I do know is the AG called us tonight and wanted a meeting, too."

"Did the AG say what about?" I asked.

I had never met Tex in person either. He had assisted on a few of my ops in the past, but only to provide intel and that was done over a secure server. Zane made a good point; if he wanted to meet in person, something was really wrong.

"Peter received an email tonight. He refused to forward the message and wanted Garrett to view it on his computer only. Garrett ran the email and found the location origin. Brace, brother. It's gonna be a long night – the POTUS, the AG, and Tex." Z stopped and shook his head. "I have a bad feeling about this."

By the time we made our way back outside, the Eurocopter EC155 was touching down. Luckily for us, this was going to be a short flight. The EC only held eight normal-size men. Both Z and I were well over six foot, and Tom's personal protection wasn't much smaller than us; it was going to be a tight fit.

Garrett was the first to rush the helicopter, no doubt he wanted to climb aboard and start scouring the dark web for information. I, however, just wanted to get in and catch a quick nap before shit hit the fan.

In under a minute everyone was aboard, and we were underway.

2

OLIVIA

Every inch of my body ached, muscles I didn't even know I had screamed in protest when I tried to sit up. My head was pounding from lack of sleep and food. The overwhelming stench of rotting garbage and... something else in the room made my stomach lurch, and I started to gag. It was hard to tell what the "something else" was with the amount of dried vomit that was now crusted in my hair. I couldn't remember the last time I was allowed to take a shower. It had to have been days, but for all I knew, it could have been weeks.

When I was first brought here, I was given a daily bath and a tray of food. After the guard had caught me trying to pick the lock on my handcuffs with a plastic fork, I was no longer allowed food, or a bath, or the luxury of looking outside. The windows were now covered over with plywood, preventing even the tiniest sliver of daylight into the room. I had no idea what time of day it was, or how many days had passed since the windows were covered.

It had to have been past the morning hours if the guards were still sticking to their original schedule. There sitting next to me was a single bottle of water and V8 juice. That's what I was supposed to live on, fucking vegetable juice and a small water.

I opened my water and took the first tentative sip, waiting to see if my stomach would reject the liquid. I would only get one bottle, I knew better than to drink it all at once even if my dehydrated body begged me to.

Yelling outside the door made me jump, and the tiniest bit of water splashed and hit me in the face. What I wouldn't have given to dump the bottle over my head and rinse some of the grime off of my face and hair. But that wasn't an option; the only water I would spare for cleanup was on my wrist. It was a waste now, I was sure of it. The angry red welts from the cuff rubbing had turned into open sores that were oozing pus. They were most definitely infected; it was pointless to continue to try and clean them. But I couldn't stand the disgusting sight and needed to wash it anyway, even if it was in vain.

The yelling continued, growing louder and louder. These fucking idiots screamed and fought with one another every day. They had to have been the worst kidnappers in the history of kidnapping. The idiots obviously knew that I was a nobody. Sure, my mother worked as a White House aide, but no one would risk their political career on an aide's kidnapped daughter. Not to mention the government didn't pay ransom.

I laid back down on the hard, wood floor and found my focal point on the wall across the room. I tried to tune out the yelling by focusing on the one blemish on the otherwise perfect black and white damask wallpaper. Most days it worked, I could find my center and meditate, other days I focused on that one spot and plotted how I was going to kill my captors.

I knew that was never going to happen and I was going to die in this room. I had made peace with it. I felt sorry for my mom; she would miss me and blame herself for my wild ways. But the truth was, she was a great mom even if she didn't have a lot of time for me. I always knew she loved me. My best friend, Erin, hell she was my only real friend, she would miss me, too. She tried to tell me I had been drinking too much, and she was worried about me. So, what did I do? I shoved her out of my life. Not because she was wrong, but because she was right. I wasn't ready to face what my life had become. What a disappointment I had turned out to be. The last conversation I had with her I told her to mind her own fucking business and lose my number.

Now I was locked in this revolting room, my death

was certain, and I regretted every nasty word I ever spoke to her. Yet, she would never know. I would die in this room alone. Either the men who took me would kill me or the worsening infection on my wrist would. I begged the assholes to switch the metal cuffs to my other hand to give my shoulder a break and let the sores heal, but they refused.

My special spot on the wall was not helping, and no matter how hard I tried, I couldn't quiet my thoughts. I couldn't make the yelling go away. I squinted my eyes and strained to concentrate on the red mark across the room. The harder I tried to focus, the more my head hurt. All the years of yoga classes and meditation techniques I had learned were not helping. Instead, my mind was wandering, I couldn't stop thinking about the spot on the wall. It had become an obsession of mine. I had nothing to do in this place but think.

In all my pondering, I had gathered that this room was freshly wallpapered. I knew it was. The first day I was brought here I could smell the glue. Why in the hell would someone wallpaper a room to keep a hostage in? I was beginning to think they chose this ugly pattern to drive me crazy. It made me dizzy just looking at it. Now there was a red spot across the room. Either I had officially lost my mind, or it was getting bigger every time I looked at it.

Gunshots pulled me from thoughts of wallpaper

and spots. I crawled to the wall as quickly as I could and balled myself up as small as possible. I prayed to God that the assholes who took me were out there killing each other. I strained to hear what was being said. I spoke very little Spanish and could only pick up on certain words. I knew the asshole who took me could speak English. He spoke it fluently the night I met him in the bar. We spoke for a long while, his English was perfect. Now, however, the bastard wouldn't speak a word of it to me. He only spoke in Spanish like the rest of them.

I was going to die locked in this room.

3

LEO

When we touched down, Z received a message from Tex with coordinates to a place he called the Diner. When we arrived at the nondescript location in the middle of nowhere, it was indeed an abandoned restaurant.

"Sir, I have to advise against this. The location has not been vetted or cleared," Gerald said, clearly vexed by the whole trip.

"Nonsense. I'm fine," Tom dismissed.

"Sir."

"I said I was fine Gerald. End of," Tom asserted.

With that, we all exited the SUV that was helpfully left for us at the airstrip. "Mr. President, if you wouldn't mind standing back with Gerald while I clear the building," Z proposed even though Tom had just given Gerald a hard time about not entering.

This was not our first rodeo with the President. I actually felt bad for Gerald and Aaron; it had to be difficult guarding the POTUS when he made a habit of going off the reservation.

"Jesus, how many times do I have to remind you all – Tom, just Tom. There is no press corps here, no White House staff. We are gathered here as friends," the President corrected. "And are you all forgetting that I was a UDT, doing the business in dungarees before the word SEAL was even thought up? Fuckin' SEAL pups."

It was hard to contain my laughter at Tom's outburst reminding us all that he was an original Frogman. The Underwater Demolition Team, or UDTs, pioneered Naval Special Warfare. It is because of them that NSW is what it is today. They were badass motherfuckers with green faces wreaking havoc in Vietnam, and any Special Operator current or former knows to respect a UDT's place in SEAL history. Tom was the only person that could get away with calling Z a SEAL pup. It was downright hilarious. I was definitely saving that shit for later use. Though there was no doubt it would earn me an ass chewing, it would be well worth it.

Tom pulled a Sig Sauer P226 from his concealed holster under his suit jacket and leveled it at the door. "Now if you boys are done yapping your gums about my safety, let's get this show on the road."

"Hooyah," Z barked out a laugh.

Gerald and Aaron took point, breaching the front door first, followed by Garrett and the Attorney General. Tom was close behind them, his sidearm still at the ready. Zane had his six, his own firearm drawn. I pulled up the back.

"Come on back," a voice called out in a thick southern accent from behind the old school swinging diner doors that led to the kitchen.

A man I assumed was Tex stood from a makeshift workstation when we entered, five guns pointing in his direction. "Still an over-cautious SOB, I see."

"Trust but verify, old friend. Are we secure?" Z asked.

I scanned the room and noted the large topographical map on the stainless-steel chef's station, and three of the five monitors had intel reports and maps on their screens. The other two were surveillance footage of both the outside of the diner and the airstrip where we landed.

"We are," Tex answered. "Thanks for making the trip down here. Sorry for the trouble, but there are some things I will not discuss even over the most secure line." Tex stood up a little straighter and squared his shoulders, blatantly noticing the President was in the room. "Mr. President."

"John Keegan. It is a pleasure to finally meet you, I have heard a lot about you. And, it's Tom, please."

"Yeah, I don't think that is going to happen, sir," Tex chuckled.

"I really wish all of you would learn to call me Tom when we're in private." The President sighed. I couldn't help but crack a smile. I could still remember the first time the President scolded me and demanded I call him Tom, instead of Mr. President. I thought it was a joke. No one in their right mind would call the POTUS by his first name. But sure as shit, that's what Tom wanted to be called.

"Tex, this is Panther." Z pointed to me and continued with the introductions. "Gerald and Aaron, Tom's detail. Garrett, my in-house intel specialist, and the AG, Peter Newton."

Tex gave a chin lift in response. He glanced around the room, his eyes taking each of us in. No doubt sizing us up. Once a SEAL always a SEAL. Just because a man leaves the teams doesn't mean his training goes away. We all may be on the same side, but a man can never be too careful.

"Now that introductions have been made, whatcha got for us?" Z asked.

Unfortunately, Garrett's in-flight search came up with nothing. We were all interested in what Tex had found.

I studied the map on the table and noted the Potomac River was to the West, the Chesapeake Bay to the East, and sandwiched between the two bodies of water was Scotland, Maryland, approximately eighty miles south of Annapolis. However, nothing on the map indicated an exact location.

"I actually stumbled on something by accident. I was in a chat room looking into an information broker when there was chatter about Pamela Cox and her daughter Olivia. After Zane put out on the wire that Olivia was missing, I've been keeping an eye out."

"When was this?" I asked.

"A few hours ago," Tex answered. "I would normally call it in and continue to track, but there was also chatter about the First Lady."

"What about my Rissa?" Tom growled.

"Private emails between her and Pamela Cox were hacked," Tex explained.

"The fuck you say?" Z exploded. "Garrett find the hole."

"I already did. It was an inside job. It came from an analyst at the CIA, Timothy Clark," Tex continued.

"Did he leave a footprint?" Garrett asked.

"Langley," Tex answered.

Garrett was feverishly pounding on his now open laptop, his brows pulled together in concentration. He had been looking for Timothy Clark since our last op, but he was in the wind.

"Clark is no longer with the CIA; he's rogue. We eliminated his brother," Z informed Tex.

"I heard about that. Nightstalker has quite the

reputation; her work is exceptional. You've trained her well. It's a shame that Deepweb336 couldn't be converted." Tex was referring to our last mission. Jasmin Parker, the only woman on our team, had assassinated a hacker that went by the handle Deepweb336. "He was a hell of a hacker. The CIA could've used his skills. Too bad he was a piece of shit and sold out his country. His brother is almost as good as him. But he's sloppy. He left breadcrumbs. And one more thing – he was on a CIA network when he hacked the emails. If you're telling me Clark no longer works there, you have another mole."

"I want him found, Zane! And the emails?" Tom asked.

"They were personal in nature, sir."

"How personal?"

"Personal on Pamela's end. She was asking the First Lady for advice," Tex answered.

Tom's body stiffened, and suddenly the room went electric. The President looked like he was going to stroke out. I glanced at Z, and he had caught the look as well.

"Mr. Newton, you called my office this evening and said it was urgent you meet with the team." Zane shifted gears.

"Yes. I was told that if I were to ever have a problem I was to call you," Peter said. He was facing Zane, his eyes were pleading, and he was fiddling with the hem of his untucked shirt, obviously very uncomfortable.

"Let me help you out, Peter, is there a body? And if so, who is she, where did you leave her, and for the love of Christ tell me you used a burner phone when you ordered her," Zane asked.

Peter's eyes widened in shock. "No! No, body. No prostitute," Peter spit out as if the mere word disgusted him. "As I told Garrett, I received an email at eleven this evening. At first, I thought it was a joke, but then the sender made reference to a name that had been redacted out of all SITREPs and briefings I've given to the Department of Justice. Me, I personally wrote the report and blacked out the name. The only copy of that report without the name redacted was hand delivered by me to the President, and the digital copy is in my personal safe." Peter stopped and glanced at the President.

Tom shot a look at Z. With a nod of understanding, Zane looked at Tex for a moment and studied him. Happy with whatever he saw, he turned back to Tom and nodded again.

"You may speak freely in this room; we are a hundred percent secure in here. Zane and his team are trusted, and if Zane extends that to Tex, I do, too," the President said.

That was huge. Zane didn't trust anyone outside of the people he employed.

"What did you find, Garrett?" Zane asked.

"The location the email was sent from," Garrett offered, pointing at the map on the screen. "Scotland, Maryland. Does that location mean anything to you? Whoever sent the email is not high-tech. There was no rerouting, nothing sending me on a hunt around the globe tracking down IPs and proxies. He is either a high school kid, or it is a trap. No one makes a ransom demand and gives you their location."

"Is that what this is? A ransom demand? What did they take?" Zane asked.

I am sure Zane had already mentally gone through Peter Newton's bio, too. He was a widower, no children, parents deceased.

"The email says they have my daughter," Peter announced. "But I don't have children. Whoever sent this email sent it to the wrong person. But, the fact remains, someone knows a high-value target's name, and they know I have him in custody. Not to mention someone's daughter might've been taken."

Something wasn't adding up. There was not a chance in hell someone would try and extort money or information from the Attorney General of the United States without first knowing what they took did indeed belong to him.

"Motherfucker! We need to break for about thirty minutes. Zane, I need you out front." Tom made his way to the swinging door and shook his head at his security detail. "I need privacy."

"What do you know, Tom?" Peter demanded.

Tom stopped and looked at Peter. "You have a daughter. Olivia Cox is yours."

"Pamela lied to me?" Peter whispered. "I asked her when she came home from Europe with a baby. I asked if she was mine. She said that she had met someone in Paris."

"I'm sorry, Peter. She lied, Olivia is yours," Tom said.

"What did the email say?" Peter asked Tex.

"Sir?" Tex looked at Tom. Tom nodded and looked down at his feet. If I had to bet, Tom already knew what was in those emails. "Pamela is ill. She and the First Lady were discussing Pamela's will and trust. She was also asking the First Lady her opinion on how to introduce Olivia to you. She wanted to make things right before she got any worse. I have to say, I agree with Garrett on this one. It was too easy to trace the hack. Something isn't adding up. The hack came from Langley, but all the chatter came from Scotland, Maryland."

Goddamn. This just kept getting more and more complicated. Peter stood silently, his stare devoid of any emotion. He looked like a man that had just had his world torn apart. I felt bad for the man, finding out that the woman he loved lied to him and kept his child from him had to be devastating.

"We'll get her back, Peter," Tom said. "Tex, thank you for all your help. Gerald will give you my personal line. If you ever need anything in the future, you call me direct. I owe you a marker for this."

Zane followed the President out of the room and gestured for me to follow them. I heard Garrett utter a string of curse words. I would bet my ass he was trying to dig up whatever information he could. Garrett was an information junkie and world-class hacker. Leaving him and Tex alone in a room together might be dangerous. There was no doubt the two of them could take the U.S. to DEFCON one in two point five seconds.

"Do I need to call in the rest of the team now?" Zane asked when he stopped in front of Tom.

"Yes. I need them five minutes ago." The President lowered his voice. "I need a marker on this. Completely off the books. If any of this gets out, it will be a political disaster. Whoever has Olivia has the name of a man that the United States has denied any knowledge of. I *personally* denied any knowledge of his capture or detainment."

"Anything you need," Zane answered without hesitation.

4

OLIVIA

"Clear." I heard yelled outside of my door.

A few seconds later, I heard more shots ring out. I strained and listened to see if I could hear more English.

"All clear, Viper," the voice said.

The door was slowly opening, and my heart was jumping out of my chest. I held my breath and readied myself for a fight. Unless one of them shot me from across the room, I was going to claw his eyes out and rip his balls clean from his body. If I was going to die anyway, I might as well inflict maximum pain in the process.

In stepped the largest figure I had ever seen. He was completely dressed in black, face covered with a black mask, black military looking rifle pointed in my direction. I was frozen stiff. I didn't know what to do, what to say. I thought about playing dead, maybe he would just close the door and leave me there.

It had to have been only seconds, but it felt like an eternity as he slowly stalked across the room toward me. He had lowered his rifle, but I noticed his finger was still on the trigger. I would only have seconds to make my move before he pointed his gun at me again.

He knelt down next to me and gently brushed my crusty hair off my face.

"Sweet mother of God. Fucking animals," he muttered.

My eyes shot open and staring at me was the most piercing set of green eyes I had ever seen. He looked like a panther, all in black with green cat eyes.

"Olivia?" he asked.

Well, I didn't really know if it was a question or a statement, but I answered. "Yes."

"We're gonna get you out of here. I just need you to wait a moment for me to get this cuff off you," the man said.

"Where-where are you taking me now?" I asked.

This was not going as planned. I was supposed to be ripping his balls off. Kicking and screaming, and clawing my way to safety. Instead, I was hypnotized by his eyes, they were kind and gentle, and oddly I felt safe for the first time in forever.

"Panther, we are three minutes to out," a man said

from the doorway, "Holy mother fuck! It smells like rotting bodies in here."

"Damn, Blue, you're always bitching about some kind of smell," a third voice called out.

Maybe I should've been scared, maybe I should've been fighting, but the gloved hand on my bare arm kept me calm. He was gently rubbing his thumb back and forth on the inside of my bicep.

"Would you two idiots shut the hell up," the man touching me said. "We're gonna take you home, Olivia. Your ma is real worried about you."

"My ma?" I asked. "How? Who are you?"

"Don't worry about the how, *tesorino*. You'll be home in no time. I'm Panther, that's Blue, and that's Breeze." The two men across the room nodded their heads in turn.

"Panther? It fits," I whispered, embarrassed by my lack of filter.

Panther chuckled and asked, "Really, how so?"

"That was my first thought when I saw your eyes, that you looked like a black panther," I admitted.

"Here I thought it was because you thought I was as deadly and quick as the cat." He winked.

Holy shit, this man was lethal, and it had nothing to do with the many weapons he had strapped to his body. The sound of metal hitting the floor drew my attention to my wrist. It looked worse today. The open sores were encircling my entire wrist now, instead of just on the inside.

"I don't want my mom to see me like this." The gravity of the situation hit me all at once.

It's funny how when you are in the midst of a crisis, certain parts of your brain turn off and all you are worried about is surviving. But as soon as you begin to feel even the slightest bit safe, all the emotions you were suppressing flood you all at once.

The sob I had been holding back finally broke loose, and I could taste the dirt my tears washed down my cheeks. Panther started to lift me from the floor and embarrassment set in.

"I can walk," I told him.

"No, *tesorino*, you can't. I will carry you," he replied.

"But, I...I stink. I have throw up in my hair. I am okay to walk, I promise."

I didn't think I was really okay to walk. I hadn't had enough room to even stand being cuffed to a wall. But the thought of this big man holding me close to him while I smelled like puke was mortifying. It was the last thing I should've cared about, but I felt like a dirty animal.

"Come on, up you go. Hold that bad wrist close to your body. When we leave this room, I want you to keep your eyes closed. It's not pretty out there," Panther instructed, ignoring my comment.

Before Panther could lift me in his arms, a string of

curse words was yelled from the other side of the room. Panther quickly moved me completely behind him.

Protecting me.

"Motherfucker!" was yelled again from one of the other two guys.

I peeked around Panther to see one of the men was near the red spot on the wall. He was examining something on his black-gloved fingers.

"Did you see what was put in this wall?" one of the men asked.

Was he talking to me? Put in the wall? What did that even mean?

"Olivia?"

"Oh. Sorry. I don't understand what you're asking. No one has done anything to this room since I've been here. The first day I thought I could smell wallpaper glue, if that helps," I answered.

"We need ten minutes. Hold the bird for extraction," the man spoke into his shoulder. "Copy that."

The two men made fast work peeling a large piece of wallpaper off the drywall. One of the men kicked the bottom of the wall, leaving a hole. The sound made me flinch. They ripped chunks of drywall, making the opening larger.

"What the fuck?" One of them cursed.

"Jesus Christ." Came from the other.

They continued to pull back drywall, revealing

what looked to be a clear plastic drop cloth. I leaned around Panther trying to get a better view, but he stopped me.

"You don't want to look," he said.

"What is that?" I asked.

He shook his head in reply and maneuvered himself to block my view.

"Panther, you might wanna take her in the other room. Leave her with Viper."

"No! Please don't leave me," I cried.

5

LEO

The room reeked of piss and body decomposition.

Olivia was a shaking mess – the sooner I got her out of here, the better. Her grip on my arm was unrelenting. The girl was a wreck; her blonde hair was matted with throw up, and her wrist was definitely infected. Her pretty face lacked color and had taken on a grayish hue making the dark red circles around her eyes stand out. There was no doubt she was pretty, but right now, she was a far cry from the done-up party girl I had seen in pictures.

"Please," she begged.

"*Tesorino*, I am not going anywhere," I assured her. "She's good, Blue."

"Panther..." Blue warned.

I ignored Blue and concentrated on Olivia. "Do me

a favor, yeah? I want you to lie down and close your eyes. I'll stay right here with you."

Olivia nodded her head and did what I asked.

Now that the wall was broken open, the smell of rotting flesh was overwhelming. I was surprised that Olivia hadn't commented or complained about it yet. I suppose she had gotten used to the odor over the weeks she'd been locked in this room.

"We need to go," I called out when I heard the blades of the helicopter approach.

Breeze had the rest of the drywall pulled away exposing the plastic-wrapped body. Blue cut through the duct tape that was holding the body upright in between the two-by-four studs. We had not planned on cutting bodies out of walls. This was supposed to be a quick in and out mission. We needed to hurry the hell up and get the fuck gone.

"The package ready?" My comms came to life, and Viper's voice crackled in my ear.

"Roger," I replied. "Time to move, our ride is here."

Blue already had the body over his shoulder in a fireman's hold and was out the door. Breeze stayed behind as my cover.

"Time to move, Olivia." I waited for her to open her eyes. "I am gonna pick you up and carry you out of here. Remember to keep your eyes closed until I tell you."

"Okay," she whispered.

I lifted her in my arms and turned toward Breeze. With a nod of his head, he pulled his weapon up and started for the hallway.

"Package is on the move. I repeat the package is on the move," Breeze called in.

Fresh air hit my face, and I took in a deep breath. "You're doing great. We're almost to our ride."

No sooner had I reassured Olivia, we were airborne. The blast from behind us was so powerful it took us off our feet. The heat at my back made me wince, and I tried to roll in midair so I would take the brunt of the fall. We hit the ground and rolled. Olivia's head crushing my hand into the gravel as I tried to protect her head. We came to a sliding stop with her on top of me. I quickly rolled her under me trying to offer as much protection as I could.

"Get her to the helicopter," Viper yelled.

I had never been more grateful for my *ear pro*. Some guys don't wear hearing protection, I always did. There was a dull roar in my ears from the explosion, but nothing like what it would've been without it. I looked up at what was left of the burning house. Debris scattered over the yard, burning pieces of wood lay nearby.

"Now, now, now," Viper yelled again, jolting me into action.

Wordlessly, I scooped Olivia up. Viper, Blue, and Breeze all gave us cover as I ran to the helicopter.

The pilot was already throttling up the engine and had engaged the rotors preparing for lift off. Breeze was in behind us, Blue not far behind still carrying the body we had found in the wall. Viper, who was always the first in and the last to leave, jumped in behind Blue.

"Go," Viper yelled over the blades.

Viper angrily ripped his black balaclava from his head. It was a toss-up if he was vibrating from irritation or if the vibration was from the helo. He was fucking pissed. Not that I wasn't – that was a clusterfuck.

"What in the fuck was that?" Viper roared.

I think that was probably a rhetorical question, but Blue still answered. "That was fucked is what that was!"

"You think? Jesus Christ," Viper returned.

Olivia hadn't moved, hadn't said a word. She was so slight in my arms I had almost forgotten she was there. I didn't bother trying to speak to her between the loud cabin and the explosion – she wouldn't have been able to hear me anyway. When I looked down at her, I was surprised to see she was staring up at me. Deep brown eyes that were so dark I couldn't make out her pupils.

I gave her what I hoped was a reassuring smile. Comforting a woman was not something I was used to. Yet, as foreign as it was to me, I wanted to comfort this woman. I knew I should've passed Olivia off to Blue, he was the one that all the frog hogs called sweet. Women basically threw themselves at him the moment he opened his mouth. The man had rap, no doubt. But as much as I knew I should pass her off, I couldn't. There was something about her, something in the way she looked at me that tied me to her.

Maybe I had misjudged the girl, maybe she wasn't the spoiled party girl I thought she was. Or maybe she was just in shock and what I saw in her captivating chocolate eyes was nothing more than hero worship, because I was the one that was point. If it had been any of the other guys, she would be on their lap looking at them the same way.

The barn was only about a hundred kilometers north of our location; we'd have Olivia on the ground, cleaned up, and back with her ma within the hour.

I caught Viper's attention and pointed to a bottle of water at his feet. He passed me the water. I cracked the top and carefully nudged Olivia to sit up.

"Drink," I mouthed.

She started to gulp the water down, but I shook my head and pulled the water away. "Slowly."

I put the bottle back to her lips, and she took small sips. When she was done she pushed the bottle away and closed her eyes. Poor girl had to be exhausted. Not only had she been held against her will, but the adrenaline dump was coming.

"Prepare. Wheels down in two...one...touchdown," the pilot's voice came over my earpiece.

"Roger. Good ride," Viper returned.

Viper rushed to jump out of the helicopter, Blue and Breeze quickly followed. It took me a moment longer, careful not to jostle Olivia more than necessary.

The moment we entered the basement of the barn, there was a fury of commotion. The team started to divest themselves of weapons and gear. Doc was already waiting with a gurney bed set-up. IV poles were pushed off to the side with hanging bags of fluid at the ready.

"Set her down," Doc instructed.

"Don't leave me," Olivia whispered, with pleading eyes.

"The doctor is gonna check you out. I'm gonna give him some room," I answered.

"Don't leave me," Olivia shouted.

I glanced at the doctor then my team, shocked at the vehemence in her tone. Viper gestured for me to stay with her, and the doctor's lips flattened to two thin lines. I wasn't sure if he was annoyed I'd be in his way or sympathetic to how frightened Olivia was. Either way, I didn't give the first fuck if he was mad; there was no way I was leaving Olivia now.

"I'm staying right here, *tesorino*."

I was not good at this; gentle, slow movements were not in my nature. In the field when I needed to deposit a man on a bed, I didn't take painstaking care not to cause him anymore discomfort. I dropped and dashed. There was no time to worry if I hurt his boo-boo; I had shit to do and scumbags to kill. Sounded harsh, but that's the nature of the beast. Combat and black ops is not a place for weakness or feelings.

I didn't know how to do this, I wasn't even this gentle with my ma. She was an Italian after all. The woman was tough as nails after raising two hellions for sons and a devil for a daughter. I didn't think that woman had a touchy-feely bone left in her body. My ma was the strongest woman I knew.

As soon as Olivia was softly laid out on the bed, the doc went to work.

"Hi Olivia, I'm Dr. Westinghouse. I am the President's personal physician. He asked me to take a look at you. Before we begin, I have to ask you if you want me to clear the room. I'm going to ask you some very personal questions."

Was he nuts? Not one minute before, I promised Olivia I wouldn't leave her side. There wasn't a snowball's chance in hell I was leaving.

Olivia's eyes came to mine, panic clearly written all over her face. "I'm not leaving her, Doc," I told him.

"I want him to stay," she answered.

I wondered if Olivia even remembered my name with all the trauma she'd been through. It was doubtful. She just didn't want to be alone. But the way she turned to me before she answered the doctor hit me straight in the gut.

"Alright. Let's begin. My apologies in advance for being so obtrusive. Did anyone touch you in a sexual manner?" Westinghouse asked.

Before Olivia could answer, I felt my heart rate spike, and for some reason that I couldn't place, an overwhelming sense of protectiveness roared to the surface. A feeling so strong it shocked the shit out of me. I had never, not even with my sister or ma felt this strongly before.

"No one touched me like that," she answered.

"Good. That's good. Now why don't you tell me where you hurt, and we'll go from there." Dr. Westinghouse smiled at Olivia.

Even though Olivia had told the doctor she had not been sexually violated, the feeling didn't go away. I wished we had not taken out the crew that was holding Olivia so quickly; they deserved a slow and painful death for what they did to her.

6

OLIVIA

It was hard to concentrate on all the questions the doctor was asking when Panther's green eyes were laser focused on me. He looked like some sort of avenging warrior with the angry look on his face and his black military gear still on. I should've been scared, but I wasn't. Having him next to me made me feel safe like no one would dare touch me. They'd have to get through my own personal protector before they could take me again.

"Well, Olivia, I'd say all in all you're very lucky. You'll need a round of IV antibiotics for the infection on your wrist and a few bags of fluids for dehydration. But nothing is broken. It will take a few weeks for the bruises to go away. You'll need to start with very small, easy to digest foods every two hours for a few days until your stomach adjusts. You're a tough cookie, young lady. You'll be fine. Now, I know your mother wants to come down and see you. I was told that you wanted to clean up before she saw you. Normally I would say no, you're too weak for a shower. But if you let Leo take you to the restroom and help wash your hair, that would be fine. When you come back, I'll start your IVs and Pamela can visit you."

"What? No, who is Leo?" I asked. I didn't know who this Leo person was, but there was no way Panther was leaving me.

"I'm Leo, *tesorino*," Panther explained.

"Oh." I felt my cheeks heat. How embarrassing.

"It's okay. It's hard to keep all of our names straight." He smiled. "Come on, I'll help you clean up. Your ma brought you some clean clothes.

Wow, he had a great smile. Straight white teeth and full lips. Of course, he would. He reminded me of a superhero. Aren't all superheroes in the movies good looking?

Before I could tell him I could walk, he swept me up into his arms as if I weighed nothing. I should've protested, but I didn't. Instead, I burrowed in and enjoyed the feeling.

I was safe.

The door closed behind us, and Leo set me down on the lid of the toilet. The sound of the door clicking shut had my body locking tight. My fists clenched and an unexplainable fear ripped through my body. The safety I'd felt in Leo's arms moments before vanished and I was transported back to being locked in a filthy room. I hated the metallic sound of the door latching, closing me in, holding me prisoner.

I couldn't breathe, and the harder I tried, the less air actually made it to my lungs.

"Slow down, *tesorino*. Slow breaths," Leo instructed.

I couldn't. The panic wouldn't subside.

"Olivia! Slow your breathing." Leo grabbed my good hand and pressed it against his chest, his tactical vest hard under my hand. "Breathe with me."

I could feel him take a deep breath and blow it out. I tried to inhale with his next breath.

"Good. Now do it again. In and out, slowly, *tesorino*. There is nothing to be scared of. It's just me and you in here. No one can hurt you." Leo continued to press my hand to his vest and breathed with me until the light-headedness subsided.

"Thank you." I sighed. After a few more slow, deep breaths I felt better. "I'm sorry. I don't understand what happened."

"There is nothing to apologize for. You had a panic attack, and it is normal. It'll happen again, you need to be prepared for it, and remember when it starts to slow your breathing or you'll pass out."

How embarrassing – a panic attack. I had never in my life had one before.

"I'm the one who should be sorry. I know better than to shut a victim in a room with a stranger," he continued.

Victim.

That's what he thought of me as. I was the hostage, he was the rescuer brought in to save the *victim*. How stupid was I to think that he was some personal superhero? Like he had any connection to me at all. I was a job, and that was it. I'm sure my mom asked Mrs. Anderson to pull some strings to find me.

I needed my mom.

I wanted her to hold me, she would wrap me in her arms and make me safe. She was the only person in the world who loved me and took care of me. I had never met my dad – he died before I was born. We left Paris when I was a baby to be closer to my grandparents because she had no one. My mom never remarried. She never even dated. It was bittersweet; she said she loved my dad so much no man could ever fill the hole in her heart he left. To this day she says she is still very much in love with him. I hoped I would find that one day, a love so strong that even in death it is still alive.

"I'm fine now. I can clean up by myself." That might've come out a little harsher than I wanted, but this man was not my knight in shining armor, and I couldn't think of him as such. I was being ridiculous and wouldn't allow myself to get attached to him.

"Where did you just go, *tesorino*?" he asked.

Those green eyes were studying me again. Somehow, I didn't think he'd be as easy to lie to as the college boys I was used to. With them, it was easy to play dumb; they weren't as observant and easy to outsmart. This man was all man – sharp and watchful.

"Why do you keep calling me *tesorino*? What does it mean?" I asked, needing to change the subject. I knew it was Italian, but it had been a long time since my language lessons, and I was pretty rusty.

"It means sweetheart." He reached his hand down. "Come on, up you go. Let's get you cleaned up."

Sweetheart? Why on earth was he calling me sweetheart?

Leo helped me stand; once I was at the sink I could balance myself enough to brush my teeth and wash my face. My hair was a different story.

"I'm sorry to ask, but can you help me with my hair? I don't know how to wash it in this tiny sink."

The small pedestal sink made it impossible for me to flip my hair in the basin and wash it and there was no bathtub to lean over. There was only a small utilitarian shower stall.

Leo looked around the small space, seemingly studying his options. I was about to tell him to forget it, maybe if I just brushed my hair that would get most of the dried puke out. It wouldn't help with the smell. However, it was better than nothing.

"Do you trust me, Olivia? Really and truly trust me?" he asked.

I wasn't sure how to answer that. He'd been nothing but nice to me. He obviously worked for or had worked for the government at some point. Not that *that* made him trustworthy.

"It's not a trick question. There's no right or wrong answer."

Call me stupid, but ultimately my decision was made because when he carried me out of that shit hole of a room, and when the house exploded, he saved me. He made sure that I was protected even if that meant he would be injured.

"I trust you," I answered.

"I'm going to help you in the shower. Are you still wearing a bra and panties?" he asked.

Holy hell! *He did not just ask me about my panties.* I looked down at my bare feet and the torn hem of the dress I had been wearing since the day I'd been taken. Of course, I couldn't have been kidnapped while out jogging when I had on proper clothes and sneakers. No, not me. I was taken from a nightclub, in a dress and heels. A very short dress that left very little to the imagination.

"I'm wearing panties. No bra," I answered honestly.

"Here's what we're going to do. I'm getting in the

shower with you. You're too weak to stand in there by yourself. Leave on your panties, and I am going to leave on my tee and boxers. But I have a rule, and this is non-negotiable. I have to lock the door."

"Why?" I blurted out. Out of everything he told me, I was questioning why he wanted the door locked. I was an idiot.

"If my gun is not strapped on, the door is locked. It doesn't matter if my team are the only ones in the next room," he explained.

I didn't understand why that was a rule or even a thought. But I didn't live his life, I had never even touched a gun. Now that I thought about it, a locked door paled in comparison to being in a tight space with a man who was trained to kill. Gun or no gun. If he wanted to hurt me, the door wouldn't have to be locked for him to do it.

"Okay," I said.

"Okay to what?" he asked.

"To all of it," I clarified.

He reached over and locked the door. He was so big and the room was so small, he reached into the shower and turned the water on without having to take a step.

"Hold on to the sink while I undress," he instructed and started to remove his vest. I watched with rapt attention as he laid his gear on a small toiletry stand. First his gun and his knife, then he toed off his boots and his pants came off next. It doesn't matter what situation you're in, there was something erotic about watching a man take off his socks. He had nice feet, and those feet led to a pair of muscular legs. His thighs must've been as big around as my waist. That was a slight exaggeration, but not by much.

Once he was done undressing, he reached back in the shower to check the water.

"It's ready." Leo came to stand behind me. Unfortunately, the mirror above the sink had started to fog, and I could no longer see him. "I'm going to unzip your dress now."

His thoughtfulness put me at ease. I might've had another panic attack if he had touched me without warning me first.

I sucked in a breath and readied myself. I had never showered with a man before, it was too intimate. I preferred not to get too close to any of the frat boys I had been with.

Even over the rushing of the water, I could hear the teeth of my zipper pull apart, or maybe that was the sound of my heartbeat roaring in my ears.

"You're doing great. The zipper is down, go ahead and let the dress fall to the floor."

I hadn't realized I had let go of the sink and was now clutching my dress to my chest. It was now or never. The faster this was over the faster I could see my mom. I mentally counted to three and dropped the dress. The fabric pooled around my feet. All I had to do was step over the material and get into the shower. It wasn't like I hadn't been naked in front of a man before. Hell, most of the men I had been with in the past year I didn't even bother to get their names. Why did it feel so different being naked in front of this man?

"I'm ready," I told him.

7

LEO

I was one dumb son of a bitch.

I think the explosion must've knocked any sense I had left clear out of my brain.

Let's get naked and take a shower together?

Fuck me, I'm an idiot.

I'd like to believe that my reasons were pure, that I merely wanted to help Olivia get cleaned up so her ma could come in and see her. Pamela had to be going out of her mind worried. Yet, I had no business offering to wash this girl. We should've called in Jasmin. Not that her bedside manner was any better than mine, but at least she was a woman.

"I'm ready." Olivia's words broke the silence.

I'm glad she was ready; however, I didn't think I was. Before I could change my mind, I picked her up and carried her into the shower. Warm water pounded on my back shielding her from the full force of it. I tried to avert my eyes and not look directly down. As hard as I tried not to, I still caught a glimpse of her perfect full breasts and pebbled nipples. I told myself it didn't count because it was just a hint of view out of my peripheral vision. I had to set her down before my cock went to full staff. Just because my brain understood what this was didn't mean he did.

I set her down and steadied her on her feet. "Lean back," I instructed.

She did, and her panty-covered ass brushed against my cock. This was not going to go well. I had to hold her while she washed her hair. There was no good way to do this. Either her ass was pressed against my hard-on, or I was in front of her and her tits would be pushed against my chest. Thank God my boxers and tee were still on.

Screw it. There was no easy way to do this with the shower being so small. I pulled her the rest of the way to me, her back now firmly pressed against my chest. "Try to keep your bad hand out of the way, it will sting like hell if the soap hits the open sores."

I grabbed the shampoo off the shelf and poured some onto the top of her head. What the hell did I know about washing a woman's hair? There was probably some special procedure, but damn if I knew. I had never taken the time to shower with a woman, nor had I ever paid attention when a date showered before she left my apartment. I massaged the gel into her scalp and down through the strands, making sure I concentrated on the areas where the vomit was caked on.

"That's nice." Olivia sighed.

She was going to kill me if she sighed like that again. It was taking all of my self-control not to allow myself even the slightest glance of the sudsy water rushing over her bare skin. With her head bent to the side and my height, I would have a perfect view of her...

Nope! Not going there. I had one job to do, and it didn't include fantasizing about what those tits would look like, or feel like. It especially didn't involve me wondering what they would taste like and if she would squirm when I tied her to my bed and had her under my control.

I shook my head trying to dislodge the mental images my overactive mind was conjuring up. It had been a long time since I had a woman in my bed. That's all this was. It wasn't Olivia I was attracted to, it was merely good old-fashioned sex deprivation.

Once the suds were gone, I repeated the process with the conditioner. The faster this was done, the sooner I could get her dressed and get back to HQ. There was still a full days' worth of after action reports to file and a debriefing with the President.

"Hair's done. Give me your hand, and I'll give you the soap to wash up."

She removed her good hand from the wall and replaced it with the one with angry red welts and open sores.

"Ouch," she yelped. "I can't balance myself with my bad hand. It's okay, my hair was enough."

Fuck me. Fuck my life. I was a dumb fuck.

"Balance yourself with your good hand." I prayed to all things holy there was a washcloth in the shower.

I knew there wasn't, but I still prayed that maybe one would magically appear.

No such luck.

I reached my arms around her to her front and lathered my hands up, I placed the bar back on the ledge and went to work.

I avoided any part of her that would further make my cock stiff, if that was even possible. Her skin was smooth, and goosebumps rose every place I touched her. That was not helping my situation. I closed my eyes and mentally recited a cadence call.

My hands were moving as quickly as they could go and still get her clean. When I stopped to re-soap my hands, I felt her body shaking.

"What's wrong? Am I hurting you?" I asked.

"No."

"Am I making you uncomfortable?" What a dumb question. Of course, the girl was uncomfortable. She was in the shower with a stranger who was touching her body after she went through such a harrowing ordeal. "What I mean is, am I touching you somewhere that's making this harder for you?"

"No."

Jesus. Now we're playing twenty questions.

"Listen, *tesorino*, I'll be honest – I'm not real good at the guessing game. I come from an Italian family. When there's something bothering someone, they blurt it out nice and loud so everyone can understand."

"I'm embarrassed you have to wash me. I feel like the victim you said I was."

Did I call her a victim? "I'm an asshole. I shouldn't've said that. I didn't mean to call you a victim. It was a poorly worded statement."

"Poorly worded or not, it's the truth," she cried.

Well damn. Without thinking, I turned Olivia in my arms and held her to my chest.

"You are not a victim! You are strong and tough and survived a horrible ordeal," I told her.

She continued to shake, and I could feel the pain radiating from her body.

When she closed her eyes she explained, "No, I really am. You wanna know what I thought about while I was lying on that floor? That I was going to die in there. I wasn't trying to escape. I was making peace with my death. A victim does that. Someone strong would've fought."

"Enough! What were you going to do exactly? Do you know how many men were holding you?"

"No."

"If you had somehow gotten out of that room, you had no idea what you were up against. Did you have some weapon I didn't see?"

"No."

"Right. So, you were going to fight your way out of there with your bare hands against fifteen men, all who had weapons."

"Um."

"You did the only thing you could do. You were compliant and waited for someone to come in and get you. You saved your own life by *not* trying to escape, which would've only pissed them off. Best case scenario they would've beat the shit out of you, and you would've wished they had killed you. Or option two, more than likely they would've put a bullet in your head and not thought twice about it. Do you understand?" I hated having to impart that truth to her, but she had to understand. She was in a no-win situation if she had tried to fight those men. "Animals do not value human life. It's a sad truth. Trust me, you did the right thing. The safest thing you could've done."

"Yes," Olivia murmured against my chest. "I understand."

"You need to put that shit outta your head right now before it eats away at you. Take a minute and sort your head out, realize there was nothing more you could've done and lock it down. You are not a victim. What I meant and should've said was, I shouldn't have shut you in a small space with me after what you'd just gone through. I should've told you what was going to happen. I'm sorry." I was still kicking my own ass for making that rookie mistake. Then I called her a victim. Damn, I was an idiot. I couldn't believe I had planted those thoughts in her head.

"Is that what you do?" she asked.

I didn't make it a habit of discussing my personal life with anyone yet for some unknown reason I decided to make an exception. "Yes."

"Does it work?"

What was this, the Spanish Inquisition?

"Yes. There is no use in dwelling on the shit I cannot change. It is what it is." I answered.

"I'll try." Her voice was soft and unsure. And suddenly I wanted to make it my life's mission to make sure she didn't try, but she succeeded in putting this behind her. Which was crazy considering I had known her all of a minute.

"Good. We're done. I'm sure your ma is waiting to see you. If she's anything like mine, she's out there driving everyone batshit crazy trying to get to you."

"Yeah, sorry. Thank you for all your help and for saving me. Sorry I didn't say it sooner."

I really did have this girl pegged wrong. "You know, most women in this situation would've been freaking the fuck out by now. Screaming and crying. Yet another reason I know you're tough."

"I think I'm still in shock. Normally I'd be throwing a hissy fit because my dress was ruined and I lost my favorite pair of Jimmy Choo's. And that is embarrassing to admit. I'm a screw-up. That's the worst part about all of this. It's all my fault. I drink too much and put myself in bad situations."

"Olivia," I warned.

"No sense in denying it I-"

I pushed her off my chest and grabbed her by both her shoulders giving her no option but to hear what I was about to tell her.

"Woman." I quickly cut her off. "No part of this is your fault. You telling me that fifteen men holding you against your will for ransom is your fault? I don't give the first two fucks if you drink too much, fuck too much, and you cry when you lose your Jimmy whatevers. No one has the right to touch you in a way you don't want to be touched. And they certainly do not have the right to drug you and take you." By the time I was done talking she looked like one of those cartoon characters with her eyes bulging out of her eye sockets. "Put it away, Olivia. Lock it down, get dressed, and go see your ma."

"I'm trying," she cried.

I had no idea how to handle a woman in distress. I worked with men. We fought together, we killed together, and we drank together. Never in my time in the teams or after did I shower with one of them while they cried in my arms. My ma and sister had never cried in front of me, most of the time they were bustin' my balls and pissing me off. I had no idea what to do with this.

"I'm sorry. I'm not good at this. You need your ma, she can help. Forget everything I said," I whispered and brushed her wet hair off her face. She looked so small and lost. Part of that was my fault.

I quickly pulled my wet tee over my head and tossed it in the sink. Pulled my cargos on over my wet boxers all the while Olivia remained quiet. I dried her off. Nothing. Not a word. I held the towel up to give her privacy while she put on clean sweatpants and a tee, still nothing. I carried her back to the gurney, not only did she not speak, she wouldn't look at me.

I had screwed up royally, yet I didn't know what to say to fix it. Or if I should even try. God knows I'd said enough to traumatize the girl already. I opted to keep my trap shut and let someone else help her. Maybe it was for the best. Every time she looked at me with her warm eyes she made me feel things I wasn't entirely comfortable with. Things that were not meant for a man like me. Olivia deserved a well-dressed man who sat behind a desk all day, a safe man who she could make a life with. Not a roughneck like me who wore a bulletproof vest and carried a gun. I had to stay away from her.

The moment she was back on the gurney, Westinghouse was at her side swabbing her forearm and inserting her IV. She no longer requested my presence while the doctor was tending to her. I took that as my cue to beat feet and get away from her.

"Anything new?" I asked, when I approached Garrett, pulling a clean tee over my head.

"We got bigger problems than we had originally thought. I went over the intel Tex gave me, things have gone from bad to worse."

Before I could question Garrett further, the door swung open. One very frantic mother came to an abrupt halt when she found five pissed off men leveling guns in her direction. I'm quite sure Pamela Cox had never been on the business end of a Sig P226 before, let alone five.

"Oh. My. God," she screamed.

Five weapons were lowered, and five sets of eyes rolled as she rushed to her daughter's side. The damn crazy woman was a cunt hair from taking one. And where the hell was Peter Newton and why wasn't he keeping the woman under control?

No sooner had the thought crossed my mind, Peter rushed in behind Pamela. He looked like hell. He also looked like he had a lot to say, I'm not sure how I drew that conclusion, but the man looked like his world had crashed in around him, and he was mad as shit about it. It was a far cry from his normal political poker face. He remained in the doorway as Pamela rushed to Olivia.

"Thank God," Pamela cried and leaned over the bed to hug her daughter. She looked like I would expect any mother to look like after finding out her daughter was safe and sound – relieved.

Pamela was a beautiful woman, she was always dressed to the nines. I had never seen the woman any other way. It was as if she had a personal stylist with her at all times. Only today, she had on jeans and a wrinkled button-up shirt.

"I'm fine." I heard Olivia choke out.

"Thank God," Pamela repeated. "My sweet girl."

Olivia sobbed into her mother's chest for long moments before she wrapped her arms around her and Pamela bent over her daughter. "I love you, Mom."

"Thank God." Pamela had not moved, and she continued to hug Olivia, obviously not able to find any other words to say. Not that I blamed her. "I love you, sweet girl."

Olivia's grip on her ma loosened and her arms dropped to the bed.

"I need a minute," Olivia wheezed. "I can't... I need a minute." Something had changed, the initial relief of seeing her ma was gone and panic laced her tone.

It was clear that Olivia was struggling to catch her

breath again. Without thinking, I went to the other side of the gurney and grabbed Olivia's hand.

"Ms. Cox, you need to back up," I stated.

Pamela stood straight and squared her shoulders, obviously not pleased with my outburst. Not that I cared. Olivia had asked twice, and the woman had not backed off.

"Look at me, Olivia," I demanded and placed her small hand on my chest. With my plate carrier off, I could now feel her nails digging in through my tee. "Breathe with me."

I inhaled slowly, holding my breath for a second before I exhaled. I watched as she struggled to copy my breathing.

"That's it, *tesorino*. Slow. Almost there."

We continued to breathe slowly, her nails stopped gouging my chest, and I let go of her hand.

"Thank you," she whispered.

"No need to thank me."

How was I going to stay away from her?

8

OLIVIA

My head was spinning.

I felt like I was going crazy and my skin was crawling. I wanted my mom to hold me and hug me, yet the moment she touched me I couldn't breathe. What was wrong with me? My mom clutched my hand and guilt washed over me, she looked devastated. I squeezed her hand trying to reassure her I was okay. However, the truth was I wasn't.

There were too many people in the room, maybe that was the problem. I wanted to go home. Everyone was looking at me like I was a crazy person; which probably wasn't far off the truth. I didn't like it.

"Hi Olivia," a man said from beside my mom and her hand flexed in mine.

It took me a moment to place the man, Peter Newton. He was the Attorney General. I'd never spoken to him, but had seen him a few times. One of the perks of your mom being close friends with the First Lady. Not only that, but my best friend was Erin Anderson, the President's daughter. I'd spent a lot of time in the private residence. Maybe I needed Erin. Even though I had been a huge bitch to her recently, and I'm sure she hated me. She might be the one who would make me feel safe.

"Honey?" my mom prompted.

"Oh sorry. Hello, Mr. Newton," I greeted.

His smile quickly faded, and he looked as if he'd swallowed a lemon. Shit. I could never remember how I was supposed to address cabinet members. "Excuse me. Mr. Attorney General," I corrected.

"Just Peter, please."

Why was he even here? I glanced around the room and didn't see the President, or Mrs. Anderson. Did they send him to check on me?

"When can I go home?" I asked.

"Soon, baby. I'm going to take you home in a jiff." My mom smiled.

"Actually, Ms. Cox, that's not the case. I was told that Peter was going to brief you, and Tom was going to speak with you, as well," one of the men with Leo said.

"They did, Mr. Lewis. I don't agree. Olivia will be coming home with me," my mom answered.

"Please call me Zane. Did Peter explain the situation to you? This is not up for negotiation," Zane volleyed.

What were they talking about? I tried to catch Leo's attention, but he was looking down at a tablet with a scowl on his face, deep lines creased his forehead, and his eyes squinted as he stared at the screen.

"I don't care. This is all Peter's fault; he can fix it. I'm taking my daughter home, and none of you have any say."

"Wait. What is going on?" I asked.

"Nothing honey. Everything is fine," mom answered.

I heard Leo growl from across the room. He no longer looked pissed – he looked lethal.

"Pamela. This is not the time to place blame," Peter spoke up.

"You don't have a say. Olivia is coming with me," my mom shouted.

I was getting dizzy bouncing from one person to another trying to follow a conversation I didn't understand.

"You're right, I don't have a say. You made that happen when you lied to me. But this isn't about your lies, this is about Olivia being safe," Peter ground out.

"Stop. Both of you. This is absolutely not the time for this," Leo scolded my mom and Peter.

"Someone better tell me what is going on," I demanded.

"Nothing," my mom said, placing her free hand over our clasped hands, holding mine in both of hers.

"There's been another threat," Leo told me at the same time.

"About me?" I asked Leo.

"Everything is fine, honey," my mom tried to speak, but Leo spoke over her. "Yes. There is new intel. The same man that is behind the first kidnapping has made new threats and more demands," Leo explained.

"She doesn't need to know this..."

Leo cut my mom off again, "You're wrong, Ms. Cox, Olivia absolutely needs to know this. I don't give a fu...I don't care about your family drama, or who you need to blame. This is about Olivia's safety and national security. You being told Olivia was being placed in protective custody was not a request. It was merely a courtesy."

"Who are you?" my mom screeched.

"I'm the man who is going to keep your daughter alive."

"That's not an answer. I don't know you." My mom was red hot mad. No one ever spoke to her the way Leo did.

"You don't. But I do." I heard the President's voice and turned my head to see him standing in the doorway with his arms crossed over his broad chest. "And if Erin were in trouble, there is no one else I would trust her security with. Zane and his team will keep her safe. You have my word."

"Why is this happening?" my mom cried.

"I cannot tell you why. You have my word, she will be safe and home as soon as the threat is neutralized," the President answered.

"Can someone please tell *me* why? What the hell is going on, why would anyone want me? I'm a no one."

This didn't make sense. None of it.

"You're my daughter, Olivia. You are in danger because of me," Peter said.

What the hell did he just say? My father was dead. My mom told me he was. My mom told me she loved him and he died. My mom told me stories about how they met and fell in love, how much she still loved him. My whole life she told me stories about him.

"What?" I asked. There had to be some mistake, or I had misunderstood altogether.

"You are my daughter," Peter repeated.

I glanced at my mom, the panic in her eyes told me everything I needed to know. Peter was telling the truth. Which meant my mom had lied to me my whole life. I pulled my hand away from my mom breaking her tight hold. Anguish replaced the panic. Maybe I should've cared but I didn't.

"Oh, my God." My mom covered her mouth and closed her eyes.

"She has a right to know," Peter said. "You've lied to

both of us for twenty-five years. We've lost all those years together."

"I lied? I went to Europe for a summer. A summer, Peter. Two months later I read in the society pages you were marrying Anna Crofton. When I left, we were planning *our* wedding. Two months..." my mom was crying harder now, barely able to get her words out. "You slept with my worst enemy and married her. You cheated and lied to me. I was protecting my child."

"Mr. Newton, Ms. Cox, perhaps you'd like to discuss this upstairs," Zane suggested.

Suddenly I was no longer scared about the new threats. My emotions had slid firmly into the anger category. I didn't know what to say...to anyone. It was as if I was a bystander in my own life, watching a TV soap opera play out in front of me. I didn't think they even realized I was in the room anymore.

My chest was tightening, and I tried to find a focal point to concentrate on to slow my breathing. It had worked for me the weeks I was being held. If I could find something to focus on, I would zone out. I found Leo across the room, his eyes already on me. He looked so strong standing there, tall and imposing. His jet-black hair slicked back from our shower. He held my eyes, and the room began to fade away. I needed him to take me away from this madness.

"There is nothing to discuss. I'm going with Olivia.

If she's going into protective custody, I'm going with," my mom insisted.

I heard my mom speaking, but I still hadn't taken my eyes off of Panther. His green eyes bore into me warming me from the inside out. His nickname fit him to a T. He looked like a sexy jungle cat ready to pounce. It was very obvious he was not impressed by my mother's display. I didn't want her coming with me. The great thing about anger was it overtook the fear. I was so angry at her, at Peter, at everyone in my life that had kept this lie perpetuating, I was no longer afraid. I just wanted them all to go away. I shook my head, and Leo nodded. There was no pity in his gaze, his anger seemed to match mine.

"All due respect ma'am that is not possible," Leo told her.

"Excuse me? I am her mother. I'm going with her." Mom seemed to have regained her composure and was back to being obstinate.

"No, Pamela, you're not. Rissa is expecting you at the residence this morning. She's made up a room for you. You'll be staying with us while Olivia is gone. The team will keep me up to date. I will make sure you are able to speak with her, but you're not going with her," Tom explained.

"But..."

"No buts. It is handled. End of." Tom's tone left no room for argument. Not even my mother would be able to change the President's mind. "Now, it's time to say goodbye. There is no time to waste, the guys have work to do, and we've taken up enough of their time."

My mother's shoulders slumped forward, all the wind had been knocked out of her sails. She lost.

"I'm sorry, honey. I am so happy you are safe. I don't want you to leave. I just got you back." My mom brushed my hair off my forehead. It should've been comforting. All I had wanted was to feel my mom's touch these past weeks. I wanted to hear her voice, and see her smile. Now I wanted her as far away from me as possible. Her betrayal stung. I felt it deep in my soul, so deep, I couldn't bear to bring it to the surface for fear I would completely lose my mind. Why had she lied to me? My mom, the one person who I thought loved me more than anything, deceived me. For what? To save her pride?

All I could do was stare at my mom. There were no words for her. I couldn't tell her everything was fine. It wasn't. I couldn't tell her I wanted to stay with her because I didn't. I refused to be the liar she was and spout out platitudes out of obligation to make her feel better.

Instead, I addressed Tom. "Mr. Anderson, can you please do me a favor and tell Erin I'm sorry. I was horrible to her, and she didn't deserve it. And please tell her she was right about everything. She'll know what I'm talking about."

"Sure will, kiddo. She misses you something fierce. I got the hot side of her tongue when I told her she couldn't see you. My Erin is a firecracker when she doesn't get her way." Tom's face always lit up when he spoke of his daughter. She was his pride and joy. Something I never had – a dad who loved me so much his face brightened when he thought of me. My mom had stolen that from me.

"Don't I know it." I laughed. I could picture Erin stomping her foot at her dad when he told her no.

"Olivia, please talk to me," my mom pleaded.

"Nothing to say," I answered.

"I'm sorry. I'd like to explain," she offered.

Peter and Tom had moved to the doorway and started talking amongst themselves. I could see Zane and the guys by the far wall trying to look like they were working. Studying tablets and a large paper map that was spread out on the desk. Everyone seemed to be trying their best to pretend not to be listening to my mom and me. Everyone except Leo. His focus had not shifted from me. He was waiting to swoop in and rescue me if needed.

Not this time.

"Mom, I don't want to hear your excuses."

"I didn't say excuses, I said I wanted to explain," she retorted.

"A little too late to explain. You lied to me my

whole life – I don't want an explanation. I want you to leave."

"You can't mean that, honey. I know you've been through an ordeal and you're scared but..."

"No, Mom, I do mean it. Leave. I've heard enough. You're a liar. You lied to me, you lied to Peter, and you probably lied to some poor guy in Paris trying to pass me off as his love child before he died," I spat out.

The look of shock on my mom's face would've been heartbreaking if I wasn't so mad. I had never spoken to her with such blatant disrespect.

"There was no other man. There never was. I have only ever been with one man, and that is your father. I fell in love with him the moment I met him and have loved him every moment since."

"Well, there is that. At least there was a sliver of truth in your momentous lie."

"Olivia," my mom cried.

"Enough, *tesorino*," Leo whispered.

"Umph." I crossed my arms over my chest like a child, uncaring about the IV in my arm. I was a grown woman being scolded by a man I barely knew. The nerve of him. It wasn't enough, not nearly. I had plenty more to say to my mom.

"I love you, honey. Be safe." And with that, my mom left the room with tears in her eyes.

I'm not sure if my disappointment stemmed from her leaving before I could spew more venom her way, or if she didn't care to stay and fight for me. Either way, she was gone. Peter following closely behind, no doubt to continue their unfinished drama in private. Good for him, I hope he gave her an earful.

The door shut behind my *parents*. The word was foreign to me. I'd never had parents, plural; I had only ever had a singular parent.

"Everything will be fine," Leo reassured me.

"Famous last words."

Nothing would ever be fine again. The days following only proved me right. My life as I knew it would be forever changed, my life would be altered in a way I could never imagine. My regrets piled up, and no amount of begging and praying could exonerate me.

9

LEO

Well, that was a clusterfuck of epic proportions. Olivia kept taking one hit after another, yet she continued to put on a brave front. After the bomb Peter had dropped on her and her ma's come apart. Olivia turned her gaze to me. I felt the weight of her stare as it hit me square in the chest. She was looking to me for support. What I wouldn't have given to scrap this mission and whisk her away someplace safe where nothing could touch her. Anywhere to get her away from the present danger and family drama I knew was hurting her more than she wanted the rest of us to see.

Westinghouse was back by Olivia's side checking her IV and her wrist again. White bandages lay on the gurney next to her as he prepared to dress her wound.

"This dressing needs to be changed once a day. I'm leaving enough sterile gauze for fourteen days. Her antibiotics are here, instructions are written out." Westinghouse held up a bottle of pills. "These start tomorrow. Small meals, lots of fluids. A minimum of 6 ounces of the electrolyte solution every hour. No pure water for the first twenty-four hours. If she is not able to keep down fluids, or she is not urinating every hour, or her urine is brown or discolored, you are to call me," Westinghouse instructed. "Zane's team will take good care of you, young lady. I'm sure of it, or I wouldn't be leaving you in their care. Lots of rest, you hear me?"

"Yes, sir. Thank you," Olivia answered.

"You're very welcome." Westinghouse turned to Tom. "Mr. President."

Tom took the doctor's outstretched hand. "Westy, thanks for all your help. We'll be in touch."

Once the doctor left the team went on alert, it was time to plan an op. We didn't have time to mess around, the Bolivians were already two steps ahead of us.

Zane had his phone out and was already dialing. "Secure line nine. Call back in five. Stand by,"

"Copy, sir," Rena's voice came over the speakerphone. Z's personal assistant was a saint. She was used to Z's curt orders.

Zane slid his finger across the screen to disconnect without further instruction and tossed it on the desk.

Z was silent for a moment, I knew he was weighing his options. This was new territory for us. We had a civilian in the room that couldn't be out of our sight. That made planning an op and speaking freely difficult.

"Olivia, we need to talk," Zane started, obviously having made his decision. Tom nodded his approval and Z continued. "You're going to hear and see things that you shouldn't. However, it's unavoidable. You're not to share any of it with anyone. Not your mother, not Peter, or Erin. Not any fucking person outside of this room. Are we clear?"

"Yes."

"Crystal clear? This is not a game. You talk, people die, and that will be on you."

Olivia's face paled, and she looked at Tom.

"What Zane is so eloquently trying to say is." Tom's tone was laced with condemnation. He didn't like the way Zane was talking to Olivia any more than I did. "Is that it's important that you never speak about any of this. Not your kidnapping, not anything you may hear. And you are not to try and contact anyone while you're gone. I will be the only person outside of this room who knows where you are. It has to be this way, kiddo. I know it is scary and confusing. I wish there was another way. But you cannot be left unprotected."

"Crystal clear," she whispered, her voice shaky. I wanted to throat punch Z for scaring her even more than she already was.

Tex's latest intel showed the Bolivians had more

information about Peter Newton, Pamela Cox, and Olivia than we'd originally thought. They had been gathering information and planning this for months. The house we were led to was indeed a trap. Not that we hadn't already known that and prepared for it. The body in the wall? A fucked-up gift from the cartel. Timothy Clark, our missing CIA analyst; further showing us they'd been watching the team as well.

Zane's phone vibrated on the desk, and he picked it up. "We good?" he asked.

"Roger," Tom answered.

Zane entered his security code to unlock his phone and answered, "Go."

"Crash code of the day – Napa sixer," Rena answered.

"Where's Jake?" Z inquired.

Jake was another analyst employed by Z Corps. He and Garrett were our information specialists. If we needed intel, they found it.

"Here, Z," Jake came on the line.

"Mission shift. I need everything you can find on Gomez and any known associates. I want everything from his Capos and Lieutenants to his runners and territory leaders. Dig so far up his ass it hurts. And I want him to know we're doing it. Leave him a trail. I need him to scramble. Start the kill chain and plant doubt." Zane stopped for a moment and turned to

Tom. "I am going to ask you to leave the room for a moment. Plausible deniability."

"No," the President answered.

"Tom, you need to leave the room. You asked me to take care of this. And I will, but it won't be ethical and it won't be legal. You have to leave," Zane tried again.

"Boy, when have I ever left your balls hanging in the wind? Never. And I won't start now. You may speak freely." Tom wasn't going to back down. Zane always gave him the option to leave the room, but Tom never took it.

"I need a thumb drive that is in the AG's personal home safe. Send in the Blue Team to retrieve it," Zane instructed.

"A little B and E, they'll be pleased. Anything else?" I could hear Jake's fingers clicking on his keyboard as he waited.

"All information is to be sent to Garrett, SAT COMM one. Red is black. All communication is B230. Operation dirt diver is a go," Zane finished.

"Copy that." Jake disconnected.

"Rena?"

"Yes, sir, I know your fish. I'll take care of them. Blue Team has been alerted, and all calls are forwarded to me. Hope you enjoy your vacation in Hawaii. You'll be at the Aloha hotel spending ungodly amounts of money on Mai Tais. What should I do about Nightstalker and Ghost?" Rena was damn efficient. She ran every aspect of Zane's life down to his fish tank in his office.

"They've been taken care of." Before Rena could respond, Zane had disconnected the call. Bastard always had to have the last word.

"Jasmin will be here in a moment. She went to Olivia's apartment and packed some things. She also grabbed your go bag from the office." Zane turned back to the map.

"Is he always so bossy?" Olivia asked me.

"Yes, *tesorino*, he is." I couldn't help but laugh at her question.

Zane was hard to handle if you didn't know him. He came off as a dick most of the time because he gave zero fucks if he offended someone and he was no-nonsense. But he would give his life to save a stranger. There was a reason he was the way he was. He was a warrior who led warriors. He had taken on a responsibility that most men couldn't begin to fathom. Zane had seen and done things that left him scarred and broken. He lived behind a fortress so tall and impenetrable it was a wonder he could still function daily. Yet, he was the best operator I knew. Even though I was pissed he had kept family secrets from me, I still trusted him with my life. There was no other man I would follow into battle.

The perimeter alarm sounded, and I glanced at the monitor in time to see a flash of a matte black Honda

CBR1000 race by. Jasmin was here. If Olivia thought Zane was bossy, then she was in for a treat meeting Jasmin. There was no way to explain Nightstalker; she was as badass as they came. She earned her spot on the team, there were no handouts when it came to this woman. She could outshoot most of us and was notorious for training with an extra ten to fifteen pounds in her ruck to prove she was up to date on the men's standards.

The door slowly pushed open, and the first thing that came into view was the dark earth barrel of Penelope, Jasmin's P226. Yes, she named her weapon. And if you juiced her about it, she'd cut your ass down to size.

"Yo," she greeted.

"Nice, Jassy." I laughed. "You sure know how to enter a room."

"What? A girl can never be too careful. Just because you fuckers can see who is at the door doesn't mean I can see in. You never know."

So it begins.

Jasmin was notorious for her mouth. She cursed like a sailor. Only she wasn't, she was Army Human Intelligence. She was so good at her job the Army had lent her out to other special forces teams. After a mission was complete, it was her job to go in and collect intel. It didn't take long for the CIA to catch on and recruit her, too.

"And stop calling me, Jassy." She hated that nickname. All the more reason for me to continue to use it.

"I got your go bag." Jasmin turned her attention to Olivia who looked like she was about to jump out of the bed and run. "You must be Hash. I packed you some stuff for your trip. Nice digs by the way."

"Hash?" Olivia questioned.

"Sorry, the guys didn't tell you. Your callout. We can't use your real name over comms. You're Hash."

"Why Hash?"

"Girl, you use more hashtags on your social media posts than I've ever seen. I didn't know there *were* so many hashtags," Jasmin explained. "Even in your private messages, you use them."

Olivia's face pinkened, a pretty blush covering her cheeks. She looked so much younger than twenty-five. She could've easily passed for eighteen, which made me feel like even more of a douche for lusting after her. She was still a kid.

"Thanks for grabbing my stuff. You didn't have to do that." Olivia yawned. "Sorry."

"No trouble at all. Hey, Uncle. Long time no see." Jasmin turned to Tom.

It was still hard to wrap my brain around the President being Jasmin's uncle. She was devastated when she found out her family history had been kept a secret, and after her parents were killed, she was sent to live with a close friend of theirs, not her uncle. Tom kept his promise to his sister and brother-in-law and didn't tell Jasmin about the family connection until just a few weeks ago. They were slowly getting to know each other and healing from the deception. I suppose a lot of it had to do with Linc, Jasmin's husband. Jasmin did not forgive easily and never forgot. But Linc had urged her to forge a relationship with Tom. Between that and Tom standing behind her when Linc got captured and was thought to be dead, things were starting to look up for them. Tom had helped her search for Linc. She never gave up hope he was alive, even when the rest of us had.

"Hello, sweetheart. How is Linc?" Tom asked.

"Still a sexy pain in the ass. He hates sitting behind a desk and wants to get back in the field. I guess we're running comms on this op. I don't want to leave him unattended," Jasmin answered.

It was so nice to see her happy. The last two years she had been miserable. Linc was all she needed to smooth all her broken, jagged pieces. In this line of work, none of us would ever be whole, it was impossible; we knew too much and carried out missions disposing of the worst scumbags the world had to offer. Yet, I would imagine having the love of a good woman to come home to would make it a little easier. I didn't know for sure, I'd never had it. But seeing Linc and Jasmin gave me hope. Something I never thought I'd have. Hope that one day I could have that, too.

"Jas, Jake's been briefed. I may need you to run

intel to Tex if Jake gets overloaded. Tex offered, and as much as I hate to outsource this, there's no other person I'd trust. He's expecting you. Please keep him appraised of the crash code until further notice. And for the love of Christ, keep my brother in line," Zane ordered.

"Copy that. I already have the handcuffs out," Jasmin quipped.

"Stop talking." Z smiled.

Z has always had a soft spot for Jasmin. I guess in some small way we all did. She was the little sister we could all pick on. And Jasmin gave as good as she got.

"Alrighty. With that, I'm going to the office. You all be safe. Call me if you need anything, I'll be on stand-by." Jasmin started for the door when she stopped and turned back to Olivia, her voice gentling in a way I'd never heard before. "I heard about your mom and Peter Newton. The men in this room will tell you that they don't think I have a girly bone in my body or feelings, and they may be right. But the truth is I know what this cut feels like. It is deep and ugly and will eat you up inside. I guess what I'm trying to say is if you need to talk, reach out. Don't let this fester in you."

"Thank you, Jasmin." Olivia averted her eyes and started to fidget with the hem of her tee. She looked nervous and still on edge. I needed to get her away from the commotion of the room. Not that any of the other guys had spoken to her. It still had to be nerve-wracking to have five men circling around you.

"*Tesorino*, I'm going to take out your IV now so we can hit the road." I didn't wait for her to acknowledge me before I got to work.

"Zane. I'm walking my niece out, and I'm sure Gerald and Aaron are ready to have a coronary by now. It burns my ass I cannot even leave my own house without a five-hour security brief. Jesus!"

"Where are you supposed to be today, sir?" Colin asked, speaking up for the first time.

"In the basement gym. That's where I am every time I need to leave without my detail. Now the hard part is getting back."

"You know people are gonna catch on soon if you don't start bulking up." Colin laughed.

"Funny guy today, eh? Keep me updated, Zane, and everyone be safe." Tom placed a kiss on Olivia's forehead as I placed a Band-Aid on the needle mark from her IV. "Everything will work out, kiddo. I trust these men with my life, and yours. I'll look after your mom until you get back."

Olivia didn't speak, she just nodded her head and closed her eyes. I wasn't sure if she was that exhausted or if she was upset at the mention of her mom.

Tom leveled me with a look that could not be mistaken for what it was. The look of a man who cared deeply for this girl and wanted her safe.

"Not one single hair on her head will be hurt, Tom. You have my word."

"I know, or I wouldn't be walking out the door. Men, Godspeed and good luck."

"We're gonna bounce, too. We've got gear to grab before we head out," Eric said as he and Colin made their way to us. "We'll be an hour behind you tops. Olivia, we'll see you soon."

"Oh...kay..." Eric and Colin both laughed at her response. I honestly couldn't remember if they had actually been introduced. They'd been in the corner all morning going over SITREPs and intel with Garrett.

"Olivia, this is Eric and Colin. They will be our backup team for this op," I explained.

"Nice to meet you both. And thank you for coming to get me," she whispered.

"No need to thank us, Hash. Listen to Leo, he'll keep you safe. We'll meet up again soon. But you need to know that just because you don't see us, doesn't mean we're not around. We got your six," Colin said.

"Thanks, bro. We're headed north first. I'll hit you with the route when Garrett finishes mapping it out. We're gonna straight shot it, the less CCTV cameras he has to disable on the way the better." Both men gave me a chin lift and left.

"How many of you guys are there?" Olivia asked.

"Zane has three teams, six people to a team. Red, Blue, and Green," I told her.

"What team is this?"

"Red."

This girl asked a lot of questions. Normally I wouldn't answer a single one of them regarding my job. The most a woman would get out of me was that I was in garbage disposal. They could draw their own conclusions from there. Being Italian, I'd had plenty of women who assumed that meant I had ties to the mob. I didn't correct them, I didn't talk about my military service, or where I went when I was gone for months on end. It was no one's business.

"I feel like an idiot not knowing anyone's name," she admitted.

"Don't. You've been through a lot. No one cares if you know their names. Besides, most of the guys will answer to asshole. If you can't remember a name, try that."

There it was.

Her first smile, and damn it was beautiful. It changed her whole appearance. She was already beautiful. However, when she smiled her whole face lit up, and her chocolate eyes caught fire. This girl was trouble.

"That's not going to happen." She laughed. "They kinda scare me too much for that."

"We're ready. Garrett is heading back to the office, and Blue and I are following you," Zane told us.

"Copy that. Olivia, I'm gonna carry you up the

stairs. When we get out of this building, keep your face buried in my chest, and your head down in the truck."

"Okay."

I scooped her off the bed and headed for the door. Zane was point going up in front of us, Jaxon took our six and nearly hugged my back. It was unnerving not having my own weapon drawn, but I couldn't safely carry Olivia and have my gun in my hand at the same time. I had to trust my team to cover us.

Zane opened the truck door, and before I could deposit Olivia in the seat she lifted her face off my chest, placing her lips close to my ear.

"Thank you, Leo."

My body instantly responded to her breathy exclamation. No woman had ever had this kind of control over my emotions. Hormones, sure. My mental state – never. I needed to keep my distance not only for my sake but for hers.

She was a mission objective – nothing more.

Or so I told myself.

10

OLIVIA

The moment I brought my lips to his ear, I regretted it.

He smelled like soap and something I could only describe as manly. The scent was unique and instantly set my body on fire. The frat and country club boys I was used to always doused themselves with so much cologne you couldn't actually smell *them*. Their scent was masked with some designer concoction. I liked this smell better.

It was hot.

I wanted to lick his neck to see if he tasted as good as he smelled.

"No need to thank me, *tesorino*," his voice rumbled against my chest.

He quickly sat me in the seat and pulled the seatbelt over my lap clicking it in place. The moan that slipped past my lips was completely accidental. An involuntary reaction to his strong forearm brushing my sensitive nipples.

Leo's body went still, his head slowly turned, and his eyes met mine. Sweet baby Jesus, this man. There was no part of him that was not intoxicating. With his face only inches from mine, it would be so easy to press my lips against his. Maybe I should drive with Zane. Not that he wasn't as good looking as Leo. All the men on the team were super-hot, but I was a little afraid of Zane, and I certainly didn't feel…*this*…whatever this was when he looked at me. I kind of wanted to pee my pants when Zane leveled his mean look in my direction.

Leo didn't say a word as he shut the door and rounded the hood to the driver's side. He remained silent as he drove us down a series of back roads out onto the main highway. It felt like an eternity before he finally spoke again.

"You need to drink. There's a bottle at your feet, it's twelve ounces. Doc said at least six ounces every hour. Try and drink at least half of the bottle."

There was something wrong. His tone wasn't angry, but neither was it friendly. Something had changed.

I picked up the bottle and unscrewed the top. "Did I do something wrong?" I wracked my mind trying to remember if I had kept my head down like he'd asked. I was sure I had.

"No."

Huh? One-word answers now. Fine. I could be silent as well. I drank the orange liquid that tasted like watered down orange drink and settled further into my seat.

"Are you hungry?"

"No." Two could play at the one-word answers.

"You have to eat. Doc said small meals every few hours. You should try some crackers and maybe a protein bar." Seemed he had something to say when he was passing along the doctor's orders. "I'm serious, you're gonna need to keep your energy up."

My mind conjured up a whole lot of reasons why I would need energy. Unfortunately, none of them were what he meant. I didn't know what it was about Leo that made my mind wander to naughty places.

His phone rang, he fiddled with a few buttons on his steering wheel, and a second later the call connected.

"Yo," he answered.

"You're clear. The tickets to Hawaii have been purchased. You have a straight shot," Zane said through the truck's speakers, his deep voice was unmistakable.

"Copy that."

The call disconnected and the radio came back on, at least if we were going to sit in silence Leo had good taste in music.

"We're going to Hawaii?" I asked, shoving a saltine cracker in my mouth.

"No."

"What is wrong with you? Did I say something or do something wrong?" I demanded.

I was getting fed up with his attitude.

"Nope." Oh, my God, I was going to scream.

"I'm sorry to put you out. I'm sure you have better things to do than babysit me and drive to…wherever we're going. But it really isn't my fault. I didn't ask for any of this. Maybe you should direct your shit attitude toward Peter Newton. Or my mother. Or better yet, the both of them. This is their fault. I'm the one who sat in that shit hole thinking I was going to die. All I want is to go home."

I sucked in a breath and tried to hold back my tears. I still hadn't had time to process that only a few hours ago I was locked in a room close to death. During which time all I could think about was my mom. I had no one now. Nothing! Here I was stuck in a truck with a man that very obviously didn't like me.

I hated that my mom lied to me. I hated that I had a dad all these years and I never got to know him. I knew I needed to hear my mom out, I'm sure she did what she did because she thought she was doing the right thing. It didn't make her lies any less painful, but I knew my mom would never set out to hurt me. Only, I couldn't do it now, I was still too mad at her. I felt like I was going to snap at any moment.

My outburst was met with more silence. He didn't want to talk, fine. I leaned my head back on the headrest and closed my eyes.

"Olivia, you need to wake up." I felt someone shaking me. I waited for the kick to come. It always came right after my name was called.

Olivia...kick to the stomach...Olivia wake up...kick.

"Olivia, wake up." More shaking.

"Please, don't."

"*Tesorino*, you're safe. Wake up."

I cracked my eyes open a sliver and saw Leo sitting next to me. He looked way madder than he did when I fell asleep. I couldn't catch a break with this guy.

"Sorry. I didn't mean to fall asleep," I apologized.

"It's fine. You needed to sleep." His voice was still harsh, but his face had gentled.

"Where are we?" I asked, noticing we were no longer moving.

"Ohio."

"Ohio? How long have I been asleep? I didn't drink!"

I frantically looked for the orange drink. The

doctor said I had to drink every hour or I'd need another IV.

"Settle, Olivia. It's fine. I called Westinghouse. He said you needed to rest and to let you sleep. Try and drink a little more now."

I couldn't believe we'd driven all the way to Ohio. That had to be six-ish hours.

"We're at a rest stop. I need to stretch my legs for a minute and hit the head. We have fifteen minutes before the cameras come back online so let's make this quick."

"Where are the others?" I asked.

"Around. Do you not think I can protect you on my own?"

"Sheesh, grumpy, I was just asking. Am I allowed to walk?"

"Yes, but if you start to get dizzy tell me right away."

I didn't wait for him to bark more orders. I opened the door and jumped out of the truck. Wow. It was a little higher than I thought it was. And I hadn't walked on my own for a while. My head started to spin, and I reached for the side of the truck to find something to grab onto. My vision was starting to blur, and I hadn't found anything.

"I got you. Hold on to me and get your balance." Leo was at my side before I could hit the ground.

Well, damn. Now I had to thank him again for saving me.

"Thanks," I mumbled. I'm sure I sounded ungrateful and bitchy. I really was thankful he didn't let me take a header, I just didn't want to have to talk to him.

"Next time please wait for me to come around and help you."

"Fine," I huffed.

He ushered me to the restroom and much to my chagrin he entered the small room with me. Once he opened all the stall doors and locked the door, he turned to me.

"Go ahead and go. Don't lock the stall door. I'm not fond of having to climb over the partition to get to you if you need me."

Need him? What the hell would I need him for? Did he think I'd need him to wipe my va-jay-jay?

Not that I would complain if he...

"Olivia?" he called to me.

"Sorry. I'm fine. You can leave now and go to the men's room.

"I'm not leaving," he informed me.

"You're not staying in here while I go to the bathroom."

"I sure as hell am. There is not a chance I'm leaving you unprotected. We have eight minutes and forty seconds until the cameras are up and functional. Hurry up."

"Fine." I gritted my teeth and made my way to the stall.

At least the toilet was clean. Silver lining. After I covered the seat with the thin paper liner, I stared at the seat. Why do we cover public toilet seats with paper? It's pointless, they don't actually do anything. Not that I want my ass on a seat that a stranger used. I prefer the hover rather than cover method of public urination etiquette. But my legs were too weak for that.

"Hurry," Leo told me.

"I am." Sheesh, I couldn't pee on demand.

"No, you're not, or I'd hear you peeing."

Holy Shit.

"You're listening to me pee?"

"Swear to Christ woman. Just pee."

"Fine."

I sat my ass on the useless paper liner and did my business. I hated Peter Newton, whatever he had done to make these men mad enough to threaten my life he'd better fix. While I was mentally making a list of all the reasons I was angry at Peter and my mom I could vaguely hear Leo peeing beside me. There was something almost intimate about urinating next to him. I shook the crazy thoughts out of my head and went back to tallying my mom's lies. That was a much safer topic than thinking about Leo.

I finished up, washed my hands, went to the door

to wait for Leo, then I used what energy I had left, and stomped all the way to the truck.

Leo beeped the locks, helped me in, rounded the front and started the engine.

"You done with your snit?" he asked with a smile.

Dick!

"No."

"OLIVIA TIME TO WAKE UP."

I cracked my eyes open and looked out the window. We were stopped again, and it was dark outside.

"Where are we?" I asked.

Leo had woken me a few times and told me to drink, but after a few gulps, I was back asleep.

"Arkansas," he told me.

He'd driven another ten hours, at least. There was a small tinge of guilt that he was doing all the driving while I slept. Then I remembered that he was a jerk and I shouldn't care.

There was a tap on Leo's driver side window. He rolled the window down halfway.

"Room 828," Zane said and passed a key card through the window.

Leo took the card without answering, not that Zane waited for a reply. He'd already turned and was walking toward the hotel.

"Wait for me to come to your side of the truck before you get out. You walk on my left, keep your head down and do not speak to anyone should we pass someone in the hall," Leo instructed.

"Why on your left?"

I'm not sure why I asked, it's not that I cared. I just didn't like him bossing me around.

"You're always on my left. My gun is on my right."

Leo got out of the truck, grabbed two backpacks from the back seat, and came to my door.

"Head down," he reminded me as we made our way to the room.

Jerk! Did he think I was so stupid I'd forget?

He keyed the lock to the hotel door, instead of him allowing me to enter first he very awkwardly walked us through the doorway together. He was huge, and it was a miracle we both fit.

The door clicked shut behind us, and he held up his left hand giving me some gesture I assumed meant to halt. He slowly pulled his gun out of the holster, his shirt pulling up the tiniest sliver, giving me a quick glance at his tanned stomach. If I wasn't so pissed at him, I would've enjoyed the peek. He left me standing at the door while he checked the room.

"Clear," he called out.

Was that supposed to mean something to me?

"You can come in now, Olivia."

Jerk.

Why didn't he just say that to begin with? When I rounded the corner, the backpack that Jasmin had left for me was on one of the beds. Leo was standing by the other bed with his backpack open.

"We're sharing a room?" I stupidly asked.

Leo stopped rummaging through his bag and turned his full attention to me.

"Yes. You're not to be out of my sight, ever. I'm sorry this is uncomfortable for you, but I'm not taking any chances with your safety."

Leo must've caught the look on my face and realized I still didn't understand what was going on. He took a deep breath and slowly blew it out. "Here's what's happening. Some bad guys took you to prove they could. Then, after they got their point across, they basically told us where you were so we could find you. Now that they have our attention, they've made their demands."

"What do you mean demands?"

"I can't tell you that."

"Why would bad guys want to prove they could take me?"

"I can't tell you that either."

"What can you tell me?" I asked.

"No more than I already have."

"Are they going to kill me?" I whispered.

"No."

"Didn't they say they were going to? Isn't that why you are trying to hide me?"

"Yes, that is what they threatened," Leo confirmed.

You hear about things like this on the news, read about it in the newspaper, threats being made on people's lives, stalkers, women who need to run from abusive husbands. But you never really think about what that means, or what it feels like to be the one running. How terrifying it is to know there is someone out there that is hunting you.

"So, I'm as good as dead."

"No. I won't let that happen."

I suddenly felt bone tired even though I had slept most of the day. I had nothing left. I wanted my mom until I remembered how mad I was at her. Without changing out of my clothes, I crawled into the bed and buried my face in the pillow.

THE SMELL of dried blood and puke filled the room. I was going to die in here. The men were yelling at each other again. I strained to hear something that would tell me who took me and why. I couldn't understand a word they spoke.

The door opened, and a man stepped in. He was filthy and smelled like liquor and cigarettes, his nasty yellow teeth and bad breath made me gag when he got close.

"Good, the princess is awake. Maybe today I fuck you before I give you breakfast. You like that princess? You like me to fuck you?" His thick accent and broken English made it difficult for me to understand him.

"Don't touch me," I screamed.

The man reached down and grabbed my shoulders shaking me so hard my neck snapped.

"Wake up!" The man's voice had changed. He was speaking English, and his tone had even softened.

"Please, don't touch me." The man covered my mouth with one of his hands, his fresh, clean smell cutting through the stench of the room. "You need to wake up. Come back to me, *tesorino*."

I struggled to push the man away.

"Olivia!"

I opened my eyes and shot up in bed. Leo was kneeling next to me looking at me but allowing me to get my bearings.

It was a dream, just a dream. Leo's here. I waited for the panic attack to come. My breathing was getting tight. Before it could get any worse Leo took my hand and placed it on his chest, he took a deep breath and I didn't need instructions this time. I started to breathe with him. My chest loosened and my vision cleared. I focused on my hand on Leo's bare chest. There were at least a dozen small scars that looked like he had a bad case of chicken pox. The more my eyes explored and took in all the scars I began to understand.

I pulled my gaze from his scars to his face; he wasn't trying to hide the look of concern that marred his handsome face. I wasn't sure if it was because I saw his scars or if it was because I had a nightmare.

"Lie back down," he whispered.

"I don't want to go back to sleep," I admitted.

In some magic maneuver, Leo pushed me on my back, rolled us both, and tucked me into his side.

"Well I do, and I can't do that if you're screaming the hotel down," he huffed, but his annoyance fell flat as he pulled my hand over his tight stomach and rested it on his chest. My breath was caught in my throat, and I was frozen in place when he didn't let go of my hand, holding it against his bare skin. "Relax. We only have a few more hours here."

His tone was gruff and his words were harsh, but his touch was soft and soothing. One hand covered mine on his chest, careful not to put pressure on my wounds. The other hand was on my hip, his thumb gently rubbing the bare skin above the waistband of my sweatpants.

I was safe.

11

LEO

I waited for Olivia's breathing to even out before I closed my eyes. This was the second time she had awoken screaming from a nightmare. Each time she did it burned my gut and made me wish I could go back and kill the fuckers who hurt Olivia all over again.

I'd been trying to distance myself from her over the last sixteen plus hours. Reminding myself over and over again not to get close. She needed my full attention to be on the op – keeping her safe. If you allow emotions to dictate your decisions, you fail. And if I failed, people got hurt. Olivia deserved better than that. She was scared and confused. I wouldn't take advantage of her vulnerability. I wasn't that man. Even if it killed me to do so. I had to keep her at arm's length. I was being a dick, but there was no other way but to push her away. She was cute as hell when she got annoyed with my one-word answers, which wasn't helping my cause, but I had continued trying my hardest not to engage in conversation.

I must've been a closet masochist wrapping Olivia in my arms to sleep. I didn't need to pull her so close, and I certainly didn't need to breathe in her scent. Funny, she hadn't put on any sort of perfume after our shower, but her hair still smelled sweet, like berries. I told myself I was holding her so she wouldn't have another nightmare and I could get a few more winks of sleep. But that was total bullshit; I wanted to know what it felt like to have her in my arms. And now that I knew, I was fucked, completely and totally FUBAR.

I willed myself to sleep. The sooner this was over, the faster Olivia could go back to her life, and I could forget what beauty felt like.

"Yeah," I answered my phone on the steering wheel, allowing the call to connect through the truck's stereo.

We'd been on the road nearly seven hours and were almost out of Oklahoma approaching the Texas border. I made sure to be out of Olivia's bed and dressed before she woke up. Neither of us spoke about her nightmare, or about me holding her all night. She whispered a thank you after I cleaned her wrist and rewrapped it but other than that, radio silence.

It had to be this way.

"Arabella has been calling your personal cell and is on hold on the office line," Rena informed me. "She said it was an emergency."

Emergency to my sister could mean anything from her losing her keys to someone being dead.

"Put her through."

A second later my sister's voice boomed through the speakers causing Olivia to wake up. "Where have you been?"

"What's the emergency, Arabella?" I cut to the chase.

"I couldn't find you," she lowered her voice.

"You couldn't find me? That's the emergency? Jesus Christ."

"I texted and called. You didn't answer. It had been twenty-four hours. I got scared. The last time...the last time that happened..." Thankfully she didn't finish her thought. Olivia was now wide-awake listening to our conversation, and I didn't want her to know what Bella was referring to.

"I'm fine, Bella," I answered.

"Where are you?" she asked.

"Bella! I'm busy, I'll call you later this week."

"Be safe. I love you," she whispered.

As much as I wanted to strangle her most of the

time, there were times like these when I could hear the care and concern in her tone that I was reminded how much I loved my sister.

"Ditto."

Without giving her a chance to ask any more questions, I hung up.

"Do you need me to stop?" I asked Olivia.

"No, thank you," she replied and continued to stare out the passenger window.

I didn't like hearing the sadness in her voice, but there was no other way.

She drifted back to sleep, and I called Zane. I pulled my secured cell out of the center console and dialed his number.

"Anything?" I asked.

"The groundwork has been laid. Hopefully, Gomez will take the bait."

"Copy that. I want it on record, I don't like this shit one bit."

"Noted. It is the fastest way to neutralize Gomez. Tex already sent one of his tracking devices to Wolf. He's expecting you and Hash tomorrow."

Tex had designed a device for his friends to use to track their women. The stories of how each of his old teammates had found their wives were legendary in our tight-knit community. Each of the men had found their other halves in what started out as a high-stakes life or death scenario but quickly turned into a true and lasting love story as they claimed their women. Lucky bastards.

"That's something."

Zane disconnected, and I went over the plan again. I didn't like that we were drawing Gomez out and essentially leading him right to us. Garrett believed the best way to get to Gomez was to have him come to us. His network in Bolivia was far-reaching, it would be like trying to find a needle in a fucked-up haystack if we went to him.

Tex had left crumbs for Gomez to follow back to us. Crumbs that Gomez, being the type of egotistical ass he was, would want to handle personally. I didn't like that we were calling the man out while Olivia was with us. He was unstable and dangerous.

With miles and miles of open road ahead of me I had nothing to do but think. For a moment, I considered waking Olivia to talk. But that would've been the equivalent of dangling the proverbial apple in front of Eve. Better to drive in silence than temptation.

ANOTHER TEN HOURS later and we were in our hotel. I was dog-dick tired after a seventeen-hour drive. I rushed through my shower, ignoring my hard cock, and threw some sweatpants and a tee on. Last night Olivia slept in the clothes she had been wearing all day. Tonight, she tortured me with a pair of rolled up boxers and a tank top. I was going to kill Jasmin for packing that shit. Surely the girl had flannel PJs that buttoned up to the neck. I made a mental note to text Garrett and ask him to buy Olivia something more appropriate to sleep in.

I walked out of the bathroom to find Olivia already asleep in one of the queen-sized beds. She looked so fucking beautiful and tempting lying there. She looked so different than in all the pictures I'd seen of her dressed up with a full face of makeup. She didn't need it and looked so much prettier without all that crap caked on. Why women did that shit is beyond me. It hid all their natural beauty.

I got into bed beside Olivia and pulled her close and buried my face in her soft hair. I told myself I was in her bed because I didn't want her to wake up screaming in her sleep. I told myself I was only there because I was tired. I told myself a bunch more shit before I admitted I was a fucking liar and fell asleep.

Olivia was thrashing in her sleep and whimpering. I glanced at the clock on the nightstand, four-thirty.

"You're safe, *tesorino*," I whispered and kissed the top of her head.

She stilled and settled in, her head tucked under my chin.

"Wake up, Olivia."

Zane had called and said him and Garrett were ready to hit the road. We had another full day ahead of us before we hit Wolf and Caroline's house in San Diego. We'd meet up with Abe there before he took us out to a cabin he owned outside of Riverton. We would stay there until this shit with Gomez was taken care of.

"Five more minutes," she whined.

"Nope. I gave you seven more minutes already," I reminded her.

This girl did not like to wake up. I don't think I'd ever seen someone sleep so much.

"Fine," she huffed and threw the blanket off her, giving me a view of her long legs. I knew what those legs felt like when they were tangled with mine as she cuddled into me. My palms ached to touch them, too. I wanted to start at her ankles and run my hands up over her calves, kiss my way up her thighs, and bury my face between her legs until she screamed my name.

Shit.

"I have the new bandages laid out for your wrist. Get dressed, and we'll clean it up."

I watched as she walked to the bathroom, my eyes glued to her tight ass. The thin boxers she wore didn't cover much, and the way she had them rolled up gave me a tiny hint of creamy ass cheek. My mouth watered, actually watered, at the thought of sinking my cock into her from behind, that full ass rippling with the force of my thrusts.

"I'm ready," Olivia called from the bathroom.

Jesus, how long had I been fantasizing about having sex with the poor girl?

I cleaned her wrist, checked the room to ensure we had everything, and headed for the truck. I clocked Zane and Garrett at my eleven o'clock as they climbed into Zane's SUV. Jaxon and Colin had gone ahead of us.

"I feel better. Do you want me to drive today?" she asked.

In a few short days, Olivia looked a hundred times better than she had the day we found her. Her appetite was back, and I no longer had to force her to drink. She was doing great. Even the sores on her wrists had started to scab over and were no longer red and warm to the touch. However, it didn't mean she was going to drive.

"No. I got it."

Once we were on the road, she put her head back and stared out her window. It looked like we were in for another day of silence.

We crossed into California hugging the Mexican

border when Olivia spoke up. "How did you get the scars on your chest?"

I might've swerved a little at her question.

"Come again?"

"Never mind. That was rude. I shouldn't've asked."

I had forgotten she had seen the scars on my chest. Thank God, she hadn't seen my back. It was a mangled mess.

Olivia turned her head back toward the window.

"Afghanistan," I answered.

"How?" she asked.

I took a deep breath and prepared myself for the flood of flashbacks.

"Routine patrol with Afghan special forces. We were up in the hills. We were ambushed, and I didn't have my plate carrier on and was hit with shrapnel."

"Why weren't you wearing your vest?" she asked

"I had just woken up. I took it off the night before to cool down. Hard lesson to learn."

"What lesson was that?"

"Complacency has no place on the battlefield. We had taken that same patrol route several times with no incident. When we stopped for the night, I felt safe and removed my vest. I was complacent," I admitted.

The scars on my chest were a constant reminder never to let my guard down.

"I'm sorry."

"It was a long time ago."

I took in the desert all around us, miles of brown barren land in all directions; it reminded me a lot of the terrain we had been patrolling. I closed the lid on that particular box and locked it back up. No good ever came from revisiting my time in the Sandbox. We were all lucky to have escaped that shithole alive. However, a lot weren't, and those were the memories I wanted to stay away from.

"Did you know that Peter was my dad before he told me in the basement?"

Shit, fuck, and damn. After two days of driving in silence, the girl sure wanted to talk now.

"Yes. I found out when we were in a mission brief before we came and got you." I was under no obligation to keep Peter and Pamela's family secrets.

"Did he know? I mean has he always known he was my dad?"

"No. From what little I heard, she had withheld the truth from him as well."

Olivia laughed. Not a shy small giggle that most girls do. No, this was a full belly laugh complete with an unashamed snort at the end. The sound was beautiful.

"Is that a nice way of saying she lied?" she asked when she regained her composure.

"Indeed."

"So, she lied to both of us. How did the bad guys find out I was his daughter if no one knew?"

"I didn't say no one knew – only I didn't know. And now we're getting close to a line I can't cross. Telling you what I know about your parents is one thing, but I cannot jeopardize national security to soothe your curiosity."

"You think that's what this is? Curiosity. Jesus, you're an ass. My mother lied to me about who my father is. You don't think I have a right to know the story?"

This girl went from laughing to having a snit faster than any woman I had ever met.

"Now, we're back to silence. You know what? Fine, I prefer the silence anyway."

"Let me ask you this? Why do you want to know who else knew?"

"Because I have a right to know," she shot back.

"You do? Or do you want to know so you can manufacture reasons to be even angrier? Which I gotta tell you, is stupid."

"I want to go back to silence."

"I bet you do. You have every right to be mad as hell at your ma. She lied to you and to Peter. What you do not have a right to do is find reasons to beat her up because you're pissed. That is bullshit."

"You think this is bullshit?"

"Woman, listen to yourself. You're doing it with me right now. I didn't say your situation is bullshit. I am telling you, your ma fucked up. She betrayed you. That is going to be hard enough to repair without you piling more shit on the heap. Don't shovel more shit. Stay on the single topic of the lie. Find out *why* she did it. And a word of advice. When you do sit down with your ma, remember that she's human and makes mistakes just like you have in the past. Remember the times that you hurt her and betrayed her trust. And then, you remember all the forgiveness she has shown you. Life is short," I told her softly.

I know that Olivia didn't ask for my advice, and more than likely I was wasting my breath. But I knew one big piece of the puzzle she didn't – her ma was sick. That was how this all started. I didn't know with what and I didn't know how bad, but it had to be critical to make a woman who had kept a secret for twenty-five years finally come clean. I didn't want Olivia to push her ma so far away they couldn't repair this quickly before it was too late.

Olivia closed her eyes and turned her head feigning sleep.

I hoped for her sake she was mulling over what I had told her – life was short.

12

OLIVIA

It had been hours since I had last spoken to Leo when we pulled into a nice, well-manicured neighborhood.

"Where are we?" I braved.

"At Wolf and Caroline's house," he answered as he pulled to the curb and cut the engine.

I glanced at the house we'd stopped in front of. There was a ginormous black SUV parked in the driveway. Either these people had a boatload of kids to cart around, or the California drivers were crazier than I thought and it was necessary to drive a tank around town for safety reasons.

"Are we staying here?"

"No. We're picking something up from Wolf and meeting Abe here. He'll drive us out to his cabin where we'll be staying," Leo explained. "Wait for me to open your door."

Leo came to my side and opened the door. The moment I stepped out Leo tagged me around the waist and pulled me to his left side. Damn, I forgot.

Before we could make it to the front porch, a man came out of the house. Holy shit he was good looking. I was beginning to wonder if Leo knew anyone that wasn't good looking.

"Panther, glad you made it," the man greeted. "You must be Hash. I'm Wolf, nice to meet you."

Not only was he hot, he was tall, too. Leo was quite possibly the tallest man I'd ever met in person, and Wolf looked him in the eye just shy of matching him in height.

"Hi, Wolf. Nice to meet you, too," I replied.

"Wolf, thanks for letting us stop by, brother. Appreciate it," Leo said as their eyes locked in some sort of silent badass communication I didn't even pretend to understand. Wolf finally broke the stare, and his eyes traveled down to Leo's arm around my waist. His face breaking out into a wide smile. "Good to know," he said cryptically.

I was about to question what he knew when a woman's voice called out from the house. "Are they here?" The woman didn't give him time to answer before she walked to the door. Wolf was so large I could barely see the woman behind him. Which was saying something because she was not short by any means. She had to be a few inches taller than my five feet four.

"Let's take this in the house," Wolf suggested and stepped aside to fully reveal the beautiful woman beside him. She was stunning with shiny brown hair that fell loose around her shoulders.

Wolf waited until the door was closed before he made the introductions. "This is my wife, Caroline."

"Sorry for the intrusion. I hope it's not too much trouble. I'm Leo."

"Finally, someone who introduces themselves by their given name instead of by their nickname." Caroline laughed. Thank goodness, I wasn't the only one who couldn't remember all the extra names the guys had.

"I'm Olivia. Nice to meet you."

"I have a package for you in my office," Wolf told Leo.

"Great, work. Let's go in the kitchen while the guys do guy stuff," Caroline suggested with a mock eye roll.

Before I could move to follow Caroline, Leo's grip tightened, and he lowered his mouth to my ear. "I'll be right here if you need anything. You're safe in this house but don't go outside for any reason."

When he stood to his full height, I looked up at him, shocked to find concern in his eyes. I figured he'd be elated to get rid of me for a while.

"Okay," I whispered.

Leo let me go, and when I turned, I found matching smiles on Wolf and Caroline's faces. They looked like they had a secret only they knew. What was that about?

Wolf kissed the top of his wife's head and gestured for Leo to follow.

"You've got to be so happy to be out of that car. Matthew said you guys drove in from Maryland."

"Who's Matthew?" I asked.

No one was supposed to know where we were. Only Leo's team and now Wolf and Abe. I wondered if Leo knew that more people knew where we were going.

"Wolf is Matthew. Sorry, I never know what name they'll use when they introduce themselves. At least Leo used his real name. Abe is on his way over now. His real name is Christopher. His wife Alabama wanted to come with him to meet you, but their son had a practice she needed to take him to."

"Honestly, I don't know how you keep the names straight. When Leo rescued me, he said his name was Panther. Then later the doctor said that Leo would help me, and I almost had a panic attack thinking a stranger was going to touch me." I snapped my mouth shut, and my hand flew up to cover it. Shit, I'd messed up. I wasn't supposed to say anything. Zane said that it was a matter of national security and people would die.

"Honey, it's okay. I know the drill. I'm married to a SEAL. Opsec is something I'm very familiar with." She must've noticed the panic on my face.

"I don't even know what *opsec* is." I thought I was about to break down and cry in front of this woman because everything was confusing.

"Come on, let's get you something to drink."

We walked into her kitchen. "Have a seat. Would you like a soda, water, orange juice?"

"I would love soda. Captain bossy pants hasn't let me have anything but water filled with electrolytes in the last three days."

The thought of having caffeine was almost enough to make me forget my gigantic screw-up. Caroline sat in the chair opposite me and pushed the glass of bubbly amber liquid my way.

"First, opsec is operational security. Basically, it means I know to keep my mouth shut. Matthew is not at liberty to tell me about his missions, and I don't ask. You said Leo rescued you, and there was a doctor involved. I don't want to invade your privacy, and we just met, but are you okay?" Caroline's eyes dropped to my wrist.

I sat and thought about her question. Was I okay?

"I don't know," I answered honestly. "I think I'm still in shock a little. Too much has hit me all at once. I don't know. I'm a mess. I want to go home so I can break down alone."

"That's the worst thing you can do, be alone. I'll spare you all the details, but I met Matthew on a flight to Virginia. I was moving there, and Matthew was visiting his friend Tex." I'd heard Zane and Leo talking about a Tex. I wondered if it was the same person. "Anyway, the plane was hijacked."

"Did you say hijacked? As in bad guys took over the plane?" I asked in amazement.

"Yep, that kind of hijacked. A group of terrorists poisoned the ice. Thankfully I smelled the poison and Matthew was able to alert Sam and Christopher and they landed the plane." Caroline stopped for a moment obviously recalling something that was unpleasant. "My point is, Matthew, Sam, and Christopher took me in and protected me. They didn't let me shrink away like I wanted to. If you haven't noticed, I'm the type of woman that most people don't give a second look. Especially three hot Navy SEALs. But they wouldn't hear of it."

"What? What do you mean give a second look? My first thought when I saw you was that you were stunning. You have the girl next door look. I'm amazed the guys saved the plane. Actually, I'm amazed you saved the day and smelled the ice. How did you not freak out? I feel like I am about to shatter into a million pieces. The only thing that is holding me together is that Leo is a big fat jerk and he keeps pissing me off. I know he doesn't want to babysit me and I really don't think he even likes me."

"Smart man," Caroline murmured.

"What?"

"Crap. What I meant is, Leo might recognize that you're ready to come apart, so he's giving you what you need in order to stay strong. Even if it means you think he's an ass. Does that make sense?"

"Not really," I admitted.

"Okay, if Leo coddled you, you'd probably have a nervous breakdown. You've obviously been through a lot. I know how overwhelming it is. Been there, done that, have two t-shirts. However, if you're pissed at him, your mind is occupied. I could be wrong about that. What I do know is, that man cares for you. I only met him ten minutes ago, but I know he does. I see it in his eyes, I see it in the way he pulled you into him protecting you, even from me. The best advice I can give you is to listen to every word he says. Do not go rogue and try and save yourself, do not go against anything he says about your safety. He knows what's best. This is what these men do. It's who they are. Listen to them, no matter what."

"Okay." I nodded my head in acknowledgment. I didn't think she was right about Leo caring about me. His job maybe, the President asking him to protect me, yes. Me, not so much. However, it sounded like Caroline knew what she was talking about when it came to me listening to Leo. I wanted to live. From what I gathered, Matthew, Sam, and Christopher had saved her from something equally as bad as my situation.

"I'm going to give you my number. I know you can't call me while you're in hiding. But when you are back home, if you ever need someone to talk to, you call me. I'll help you any way I can."

Caroline got up from the table and started rummaging through a drawer in the kitchen at the same time Leo and Matthew came back into the room.

Leo scanned the kitchen, and his eyes landed on me. The look on his face reminded me of the first time I saw him when I was locked in that disgusting room. Like a Panther ready to pounce.

"Do you have any piercings?" Leo asked.

What the hell? It took me a moment to comprehend what he was asking.

"Yeah. My ears and the cartilage at the top of my left ear," I answered.

"Perfect. Put this earring in the top hole." Leo handed me a small jewelry box. When I opened the box, it had a pair of tiny diamond earrings.

"Okay. Just one?" I asked.

Matthew and Caroline were exchanging a look between them I couldn't make out, a small smile tugged at Matthew's lips. I felt like I was intruding on a private moment between them. I wish I had that, a love so strong there were no words needed to communicate.

"There is a tracking device in the earring. If we get separated, I'll be able to find you. Tex will know your location at all times."

"Caroline's Tex?" I asked.

A chuckle came from Matthew, and he said, "I see you shared."

"Just enough for her to understand she's not alone. And yes, Olivia, the same Tex. He has helped all of us over the years. Those are stories for another day," Caroline replied.

There was a knock on the door, and Leo's hand went to his right side, but no gun was drawn. Matthew shot a look at Leo and shook his head. "That's Abe. I'll get it."

Leo seemed to relax at the mention of Abe's name but his hand still had not moved. Caroline came beside me as Leo moved in front of me positioning himself between me and the door.

"Told you so," she whispered. "That man is not going to let anything touch you. He knows you're safe in here. He knows that Sam, Hunter, and Kason are somewhere outside watching the house. Not to mention his own team is out there as well. Yet he's placing himself in front of you as if a bad guy is gonna knock on my door and get past Matthew. He won't let anyone hurt you."

I think Caroline had watched too many romantic thrillers. Leo was doing his job and that was it. Not to mention he had a woman back in Maryland waiting for him to come home, a woman who loved him, that he told he loved her, too. I couldn't bring myself to tell that to Caroline though. That was another detail I was pretending didn't exist.

"Abe, this is Panther and Hash," Matthew introduced.

"Abe." Leo stepped forward to shake his hand.

"Hi," I squeaked out. When all of this was over, I was finding the nearest military base and finding myself one of these men. Forget the weak, douchey frat boys. Military men were the way to go.

"Hash." Abe greeted but made no attempt to move closer to me or shake my hand. "Ice, how are you today?"

"I'm good, Christopher." Caroline smiled.

I glanced at her with a questioning look. She started to laugh and explained, "The ice on the airplane. After that, the guys nicknamed me Ice."

"Thanks for your hospitality, we better be on our way," Leo announced.

"Anytime, Panther." Matthew walked up to me. And by that, I mean right up to my face and lowered himself to look me in the eye. "Hash, I already told this to Panther, but I want you to hear this, too. You have my protection and that of my team. The commander has been notified, and we are on standby. Listen to everything Panther tells you, to the letter.

He'll keep you safe, and Tex will track your every move."

Matthew stood and took a step back. I couldn't stop the tears from forming. Maybe it was relief that all these big strong men would protect me. Or perhaps it was the menacing look on Matthew's face that made the reality of my situation crash in on me. I could no longer deny how much danger I was in.

"Thanks." I sucked in a breath trying to stop the tears.

Caroline and Matthew walked us to the door, hugs were exchanged, and she did give me her number. With my promise to call her, we were back in the truck following Abe.

"Did you know about what happened to Caroline?" I asked Leo.

"Yes. The nickname Ice fits her in more ways than one."

"Why's that?"

"That woman is calm, cool, and collected under pressure. A lot like you actually. She didn't freak out when that plane was hijacked. She was like ice and did what she had to do to save Matthew's life when he was in trouble. Did she tell you she was stabbed in the process?" he asked, never taking his eyes off the road.

"No." I was shocked that anyone would want to harm the sweet woman I had met.

"Of course, she didn't. She jumped on a hijacker's

back to give Matthew time to get in the cockpit. She actually fought the man. The hijacker stabbed her in the side in the process. I told you, the woman is like ice. She didn't even tell the guys she was injured. She sucked it up and went on her way." Jealousy hit me hard hearing the admiration in Leo's voice. I knew it was nothing more than appreciation for her being tough, but it stung nonetheless.

We sat in silence the rest of the way to the cabin, I was lost in thought about Caroline and everything she went through. I wouldn't have been calm. I would've hidden in the bathroom until everything was over. I wasn't strong like her, nor was I tough and brave. I wondered if the girl waiting for Leo in Maryland was like Caroline. Did she have a cool nickname, too? Hash. Mine was juvenile and lame. Given to me because I spent way too much time on social media.

The interstate gave way to side roads that turned into a windy small dirt road. We pulled to a stop in front of a small log cabin. I looked out the truck window but couldn't see any other houses through the thick evergreens surrounding the property.

"Wait..."

I cut Leo off before he could finish, "...for you to come around to my side and let me out. I know."

I hated that he felt like I was stupid and he had to repeat everything.

Without a word, we followed Abe into the cabin.

Zane, Garrett, and two other men I couldn't remember the names of stood in the living room, making the already small space look infinitely smaller with their large frames taking up most of the space.

Leo and his team jumped into action leaving me standing by the door like a forgotten, broken old toy. There were maps on the table, laptops opened, and tablets scattered on every available surface. How in the world were we all going to stay in this little space?

Abe walked over to me and took in all the men that had taken over his cabin. "Hash?" When I didn't answer right away, he tried again, "Olivia?"

"Sorry. Yes?" I turned away from the guys and gave him my full attention.

"I know this has to be a lot for you to take in. I want you to know that you're gonna be safe here."

"Everyone keeps saying that. I guess I'm having a hard time believing it. The more precautions that are taken and the more people get involved to protect me, the harder it hits me that I'm in more danger than I know," I admitted.

"We have a saying, you don't have a plan if you don't have a backup plan. The good news for you is there is not only a rock-solid plan, but there is a backup plan to their backup plan. All contingencies have been accounted for. All you need to know is you're surrounded by men who have been in tighter situations than this. Yet, there they stand."

When Abe finished his explanation, I felt marginally better. Not a lot, and not enough to calm my nerves, but a little. There was something about Abe that inspired confidence and trustworthiness. Like this man would be the person to tell me if I was going to die because he couldn't bear to lie to me. He might try and soften the blow, but he'd tell me the truth.

"Thank you for that. And thank you for letting us stay here. I hope we're not inconveniencing you," I replied.

"Don't mention it. One more thing you have to know. I want to be upfront with you. There are no secrets when planning a mission, and there is no information held back between the team. We've all read your file. That means we know about what happened to you in Maryland, your medical records, and your personal file including your family history. I'll admit there were names redacted, so I don't know all the details." I felt my face flush, and the tightness in my chest started. How embarrassing that all these people knew everything about me. "Hash, I need you to take a breath and calm down, before Panther's big ass thinks I've hurt you in some way." He stopped and waited for me to get myself under control. "I'm telling you this for two reasons. One, I hate lies. I mean, I despise them and do not tolerate them at all. I needed to be honest with you. The second reason is, I understand what you're going through with your mom. I was lied to about my father as well. I just wanted you to know that when all of this is over, if you ever need an ear, Alabama and I would be happy to listen."

I didn't trust my voice enough to speak. I needed to hurry and find a place to be alone before I cried like a weak little baby in a room full of big strong men. I had never been shown this type of kindness. Abe was a complete stranger yet he was offering to listen to my family drama. Same with Caroline and Wolf. They didn't know me, but Caroline was okay with her husband putting his life in danger to help protect me. All these people around me that were willing to sacrifice for one another only proved how alone I was. I had no friends that were out searching for me when I went missing. No one noticed that I still hadn't been home. I wondered if Mr. Anderson had told Erin how sorry I was and if she was willing to forgive me. I missed her and my mom.

13

LEO

I hadn't heard a word Z had said in the last five minutes. All of my attention was across the room on Abe and Olivia. I had to admit that jealousy was a new feeling for me. I willed myself to stay in place when something that Abe said had upset Olivia. Her face paled, and she was struggling to catch her breath. I was about to go over there when Abe said something to her that calmed her. I didn't like that one fucking bit. I wanted to be the man that comforted her. Me, and only me. I didn't give a shit if it was irrational. I had spent the last three days trying to keep her at a distance. The harder I fought it, the stronger the pull became.

"Is this gonna be a problem?" Z pulled me from my thoughts.

"Come again?"

"Swear to Christ, you'll find my boot up your ass if

you screw this up and get yourself dead, or the girl," Z commented.

"You know that makes zero sense, right?" I laughed.

"You wanna split cunt hairs, or you wanna focus on the op and stop making googly eyes at Olivia?"

"The fuck you talking about? I do not make googly eyes."

Z had finally lost his mind. Too much pressure and lack of sleep were making him see things.

"Really? You want me to get you a mirror? You're looking at Abe like you want to kill him for daring to talk to the girl. And when your eyes land on her I swear you think you're on some fucking honeymoon instead of an op. I think Jaxon should sit on her and you can run back up."

That got my attention. "The hell you will. Olivia is mine," I growled.

"Is she now? And does she know?" Z smiled. Sneaky fucker made me give away more than I wanted.

"No." I wasn't going to elaborate or give Z any more information.

"Is it going to be a problem for you? I need you focused on this op. Gomez is in the United States. Facial recognition has him entering LAX under the alias Louis Smith three hours ago."

"I'm good."

Zane studied me for a minute before he picked up his tablet and continued, "He has a three-man team with him. Tex led him straight to you. Find, fix, track, and kill. Everything is in place for you to take him out. Gomez thinks we're willing to make the trade."

"How'd you pull that off? I thought Peter was being tight-lipped about the man he had in custody."

"Blue team got the thumb drive out of Peter's safe. I could've asked Tom for the name, but I didn't want to put him in the position of divulging state secrets. This way Tom is a hundred percent clean and I still got the intel we needed. Tex and Garrett tracked Jose Siles. He was a lowly money launderer for the Gomez Cartel. Seems that Siles wanted out and contacted US officials. A low-level sweep was carried out, Siles got picked up and placed in protective custody providing he gave up everything he knew. Seems the man has more value than the cartel gave him credit for. He not only had voice recordings of meetings but his office was covered with cameras. Stills and video. Gomez doesn't know Siles has turned and wanted his best money launderer back. Seems good men are hard to find in Bolivia."

Well damn. Peter Newton would rather keep his witness than give him back to the cartel, who will most likely kill Siles, than save his daughter's life. Good to know.

"Where is Siles now?" I asked.

"Rendition. On a small island off of Iceland," Z answered pointing to the map on the table.

"How did you get Gomez to believe the US was willing to trade?"

"Garrett fixed travel documents for one Jose Siles to be transferred to a safe house in California. Those travel documents were *leaked* by Peter Newton to Gomez."

"Then Olivia doesn't need to be here. If Gomez is coming to us, it's an easy takedown, and we all go home."

Relief washed over me. It was over. Zane could take Olivia back to DC, and I would stay and take out Gomez.

"Not so fast. She needs to stay. If shit goes sideways, we need Olivia as bait. There is the one small issue with the mole that was working with Clark. The CIA wants his name. Peter is willing to trade Olivia for the name."

"Not fucking happening," I roared. "I swear to God I will cut Peter's throat before that happens." The entire room fell silent, and all stares were on me. I didn't give a fuck if they all thought I was crazy. "And you went along with this shit storm? I'll take her and run before I let this plan go down. You'll have my resignation, and we'll walk out that door. I dare any of you fuckers to stop me."

Olivia was across the room shrinking behind Abe, that only pissed me off further. Olivia had no reason to be scared of me. And hiding behind Abe, like he'd be able to stop me if I wanted to take her. She was mine, and no one was going to use her for anything. I was making all the decisions from here on out. I trusted Z, I promised Olivia she could too. I was wrong.

"Calm the hell down, Panther. Fuck no I didn't. But you think I don't know those spooks aren't following us? I know how they work, fuck, I was one of them. It's what I'd do. If we move her now, they'll know we have no intention of following orders and setting up the trade. She stays put."

"How and when did the CIA get involved? This was supposed to be off the record." When did this turn into a clusterfuck?

"Day one, when Peter's dumb ass made an unsecured call to me, and before I could shut him up the call was traced. I had no option but to play along," Z explained.

"I'm gonna fucking kill him. So much for national security. And why didn't you tell me?" I asked.

That was the part that really bothered me. I hated secrets.

"Because I knew you'd react like this. I needed you in a place where I could lock you down. If I'd told you when we stopped in Ohio, you would've gone rogue and taken her. I'm not wet behind the ears, friend. I knew that if you took her, I'd never find you."

He was right on all accounts. If I had known the

CIA was involved, Olivia and I would've disappeared. Spooks fucked everything up.

"I am holding you responsible if Olivia is hurt in any way. And mark this Zane, if Olivia is taken there will be no place that Gomez, Peter Newton, and the CIA can hide. Every last one will pay with their lives." White hot rage coursed through my veins. The thought of Gomez getting his hands on Olivia made me murderous. "Fuck!"

"Everything will be okay." A soft hand on my bicep pulled me from my thoughts. How had I missed Olivia coming to stand beside me? "You'll keep me safe. I trust you."

"You don't understand, *tesorino*. We're bringing the bad guys here to this house."

"I understand. I also know you won't let them take me again."

"We'll let you two get settled in. The perimeter has been wired, and Jaxon and Colin will be at the end of the road. Garrett and I will be a hundred meters to your west in an outbuilding. You're covered," Z clipped.

I knew Zane was pissed at my outburst. I was known for control. I never broke under pressure or lost my cool. I couldn't bring myself to give two shits if he was pissed or not.

"Roger that."

I didn't bother looking at the rest of the team as

they packed up their gear, and I didn't say goodbye when they left.

Abe was quietly standing by the door, a thoughtful look crossing his face.

"You good?" he asked.

I thought about giving him a bullshit practiced answer, the one that would be expected from a fellow operator, but this was Abe. The man could sniff bullshit out a mile away and would call me on it so fast my head would spin.

"Fuck no, I'm not."

"You know me, brother. I demand honesty at all times. But I have to admit, I understand why Viper withheld that information until you got here. This isn't a mission for you, it's personal. I get it, believe me, I understand. You gotta get yourself in check and think about this logically, methodically, and execute the mission."

He was right. I knew that I had to shut my emotions down if I wanted to keep Olivia safe.

"Copy that."

"I'm headed back down the mountain. I'm sure Wolf told you already, we're on standby if your team needs us. Truthfully, I don't see that happening. This is an easy op. Gomez and his men will come up the mountain, and you'll take them out. I read the report, Gomez wants Siles back. So much he's willing to personally come and get him. Makes me wonder who

Siles really is if he's willing to take such a risk. Anyway, try not to get too much blood on the hardwood. It's a bitch to get out."

Abe had a point. I had been so wrapped up in Olivia I hadn't thought about why Gomez would personally come and get him.

"Appreciate all your help, Abe. I'll be in touch soon. Hopefully, we can contain this to outside."

Abe waved to Olivia and left us alone in the cabin for the first time. Now that Olivia witnessed my breakdown, I wasn't sure what to say to her.

"I'm sorry if I scared you. I really wish you hadn't heard that," I admitted.

"It's fine. I wasn't scared."

She was sitting on the leather sofa with her heels on the edge of the cushion resting her chin on her knees. She looked small and young, and damn beautiful. I don't know what it was about this girl that had me so tied in knots. She made me lose all control.

"Are you hungry? The kitchen is stocked." It was past dinner time, and we hadn't eaten anything since noon when we hit a drive-thru.

"I am." She unfolded her legs and stood up. "Sit down and relax, I'll cook us something. Anything you don't eat?"

I was grateful for her offer, I was starving. "I'm easy. Anything is fine."

I took her spot on the sofa and opened my laptop.

Siles was hiding something. I shot a quick message to Garrett about Abe's suspicions and started digging myself. I had no doubt Garrett would find something before I would, but I needed to do something to busy myself.

Dinner was delicious. Surprisingly, Olivia was one hell of a cook. She made asparagus stuffed chicken, wrapped in bacon and smothered it with homemade pesto. My ma would've been impressed with her pesto, it was heavy on the garlic and perfect. We were both lost in our own thoughts throughout dinner and barely spoke. Not that it was abnormal for us. We'd spent much of our time together in silence; which made this fierce attraction toward her even more perplexing. I didn't know anything about this girl, yet I wanted to run away with her and not let anyone hurt her.

"Do I take the earring out to take a shower?" Olivia asked cutting through my musings.

"No. Leave it in."

"Is it alright if I go take a shower?" she asked.

"Yeah. I'll finish up the dishes," I offered.

"Thanks."

Olivia turned to walk away, and just like all the other times, I couldn't stop myself from watching the sexy sway of her hips. I rushed through rinsing the rest of the dishes. I didn't know if me using hot water in the kitchen would affect the water temperature in the bathroom and I didn't want her to burn herself.

I debated whether or not I should go into the master bedroom and get ready for bed myself. Somehow, I thought I was better off staying far away from Olivia while she was naked and soapy. I only trusted myself so much when it came to her. I adjusted my now semi-hard cock in my jeans and hoped that I wasn't going to have permanent damage. I don't think I'd walked around with a hard-on for this long without taking care of it, ever. Maybe that's what I needed. A shower and some self-pleasure. It would knock some of the batter off the brain, so to speak.

I finished putting the dishes away and checked the doors and windows. I was arming the alarm when Olivia joined me in the main room.

"Shower is all yours."

"You cannot be serious," I mumbled.

Tonight's PJs were a pair of skin-tight yoga pants and another tank top. Only this one had one of those built-in bra things that allowed her nipples to poke through the fabric taunting me, tempting me to lick them.

"What's wrong?" she asked and looked around the room.

"Nothing. I'll be right back. Do not open any of the doors and don't open the curtains," I commanded and left the room. Probably a whole lot harsher than I should've but damn, she was going to kill me. Maybe that was how I'd go out, death by nipple display.

I slammed the bathroom door harder than I meant to and quickly disrobed. I didn't bother waiting for the water to warm up before I stepped into the shower and fisted my cock. This was going to be embarrassingly quick. All it took was a few pumps and visions of Olivia's perfect tits and engorged nipples for me to feel my balls tighten. I didn't need to imagine what they looked like, the memory of them was fresh in my mind. Perfect heavy tits...

The door to the bathroom flew open. "Leo," Olivia's frightened voice slammed into me. Without thinking, I pulled the shower curtain open.

"Holy crap," she whispered.

I realized my hard cock was standing at attention, like a heat-seeking missile pointing directly at Olivia. It was too late to do anything about it, she'd seen everything there was to see.

"What's wrong?" I ignored the awkwardness and tried to pull her back to the original reason she had come into the bathroom.

"Hmm," she stammered.

"Focus, Olivia," I commanded and turned off the water, stepping out of the shower. Uncaring that I was not only dripping water all over the floor but getting closer to Olivia while my cock was swinging in the wind.

"Oh, I am focused." Her eyes still hadn't left my cock.

You would think that being interrupted while jerking off in the shower would make your cock go limp. Under normal circumstances, it would've. But with Olivia staring at it and unconsciously licking her plump lips my cock grew harder, if that was possible. All I could imagine was what it would feel like to push the tip past her lips... I had to shut this shit down. Olivia was scared.

"Why are you in here?" I asked.

"I heard something at the back door," she whispered.

I quickly wrapped a towel around my waist and grabbed my gun off the counter.

"Fuck. Stay in here. Keep the door locked. And no matter what you hear do not come out."

I didn't wait for her reply. I'd wasted enough time already focusing on my dick instead of the mission.

I checked the front of the house first. Nothing. I hugged the wall of the living room noting that most of the lights were already turned off. But there was still enough illumination in the room that if someone was looking in, they could see me.

I pulled back the curtain to the sliding glass back door ever so slightly. Two raccoons were on the back deck eating whatever kind of nut the large tree behind the house had dropped. I let the curtain fall and walked back to the bathroom.

I knocked on the bathroom door twice and announced, "All clear. You can come out."

The door opened and Olivia stepped into the bedroom. "Was someone out there?"

"No, it was raccoons," I answered her.

"Oh. How do you know that no one is out there?" she questioned.

"Because if someone was sneaking around the back of the house, the raccoons wouldn't be sitting out there eating."

"That makes sense. Sorry, I panicked for nothing." Her face flushed and her gaze dropped to my towel.

"It wasn't for nothing. You did the right thing. If you hear something, no matter how small, you have to tell me," I informed her.

I had to put some clothes on. It was dangerous for my cock to be this close to her, uncontained.

"I'll ummm...let you...umm...finish your shower," she stuttered.

I wasn't sure if the smile that spread across her face was because she knew what I'd been doing in there, or if she was imagining me naked again. Either way, it turned me on. I didn't give two shits if she knew I was stroking my dick thinking about her.

Without realizing what I was doing, I stepped into her space. "What are you smiling about, *tesorino*?"

"Noth...nothing." Her smile faded, and she inhaled so deeply I could feel the rush of air.

She was so beautiful. Before I had met Olivia, I had studied her pictures on her social media accounts and had drawn conclusions based on the reports I'd read regarding her disappearance. For weeks, I'd been following leads trying to find her. I had been wrong. Olivia was not the spoiled girl I thought she was. She was kind and strong. I had scoured through hundreds of images, but they all lacked one important thing. The way the brown of her eyes came alive and danced. They showed her every emotion. They were captivating, deep chocolate pools that I could no longer deny. I had tried, really tried, to keep this unexplainable attraction at bay until my mission was complete. The allure wasn't only physical, though right now, the physical pull was all I could think about. It was also the way she had conducted herself – not only during the rescue mission but every day since. I was impressed, so impressed as a matter of fact, I was done fighting this connection. I needed to see where this would go and if everything I was feeling was one-sided.

If the way her eyes clouded over and her nostrils flared was any indication, I'd say she was on board. Then there was the fact that she had been studying my dick when I got out of the shower like it was something she needed to memorize. I stopped holding myself in check, there was only one way to find out.

"Nothing? You sure about that? It looks to me like you're smiling about somethin'," I told her.

The corner of her mouth tipped up, she shrugged her shoulders, and her eyes, those fucking eyes, told me everything I needed to know. Game on.

"Do you like knowing that you have me so worked up that I was stroking myself like a teenage boy after he found his first porn mag? That all it took was a few long hard tugs and I was ready to explode? Or, was the smile because you were remembering what my cock looked like when I stepped out of the shower?"

Her cheeks pinkened at my words, and the ghost of a smile turned into a full-on smirk. She knew exactly what she was doing to me.

I was going to show this girl a whole new world.

14

OLIVIA

I was stunned into silence. Did he say I had him so worked up he was stroking himself?

There was nothing I could say. Hell, I didn't know what to say. Was he joking with me? Trying to embarrass me? I didn't mean to stare when he got out of the shower but come on, the man had a body that was straight out of the pages of a men's fitness catalog. And his... holy wow sweet mother of God.

"I've never seen..." I trailed off not knowing how to explain why I was now smiling. At least I hoped I was smiling, it felt more like a grimace to me.

"Come on, I'm sure you've seen a cock before, *tesorino*."

My back straightened at his comment. "Why? Because you think I'm a whore?"

"Easy, tiger. I meant that in this day and age with

dick pictures floating around the internet it would be virtually impossible for you never to have seen a dick before," he explained. Now I felt stupid and embarrassed. "Now, finish your sentence. You've never seen...what"

I thought for a moment how to explain and what word to use. Penis? Dick? Cock, like he called it. Hell, at this point in my mortification I was afraid I was going to blurt out the word, wiener, or something equally as stupid.

Here goes nothing.

"I've never seen one that large before," I rushed out.

It was his turn to blush. Who knew a big tough man could turn that shade of red.

"Is that so. Never? Are you sure, because if you need another look, I'd be happy to oblige." Now he was having fun at my expense.

"No really. I think I'm good. You can keep your anaconda there, in its cage."

Leo belted out a laugh at my silly description of his dick. He was beautiful, which seems like an asinine thing to call a man, yet he was. His dark hair and olive skin contrasted with his green eyes. He had it all. A rock-hard body, chiseled features, and a gigantic cock. The woman waiting for him back home was lucky. Guilt washed over me, I wasn't that type of girl. I never even flirted with another woman's man. That was a no-go for me. I might've drank too much and partied a lot, too hard most of the time, but I'd never poached another girl's boyfriend. I didn't think Leo was serious about what he was doing in the shower, I think that was his twisted way of cutting the tension. He didn't strike me as the type of man that would cheat. Maybe he was testing me to see if I was trustworthy.

"Get into bed. It's been a long day. I'll be right back."

He disappeared into the bathroom, and I turned down the comforter on the king-sized bed. I was almost positive with the threat of Gomez coming our way he'd want to stay in here with me. Not that I minded, as a matter of fact, there was no way I was going to sleep unless he was in here with me.

I slipped into bed and waited for him to come out. My thoughts immediately went to my mom. I missed her. The more I thought about what Leo said in the car he was right. I didn't need to find more things to be upset about, I only had to find a way to forgive her. I wonder if she and Peter had spoken. She had always told me she was still in love with my dad. Was that part a lie, too? Or had she spent the last twenty-five years loving a man who was alive but lost to her. Suddenly I felt a deep sadness for my mom. Peter, if I remembered correctly, had been married to a horrible woman. That must've killed my mom to know. She had to have had a good reason for keeping me from Peter all these years.

The only thing I didn't understand is how her secret came out. And why now.

Leo got into bed beside me and pulled the covers up to his waist. I turned in his direction and propped myself up on my elbow. It was so hard not to reach over and run my hand over the muscles on his stomach. The only thing stopping me was knowing he was taken.

"How does your girlfriend feel about your job?" I blurted out. *Real smooth, Olivia.* Way to make yourself look like even more of an idiot. "I mean it must be hard for you both with you gone all the time."

"Come again?"

"Your girlfriend back in Maryland. Is it hard for her when you travel?"

"Why do you think I have a girlfriend?" he asked.

Well damn, I didn't know what to say now.

"The girl you talked to on the phone, Bella. She told you she loved you, and you said it back," I explained.

"Arabella is my baby sister," he huffed, his face hardening. "What kind of man do you take me for? Do you think I would've taken you into a shower and washed you if I had a woman? Or I would've spent the last two nights in bed with you wrapped in my arms. And if that wasn't enough, you think I would jerk off thinking about you if I had a woman I loved waiting for me at home? The fuck, Olivia? And let's not forget I was willing to quit my job and go on the run to keep you safe."

Holy shit, he was beyond pissed.

"I wasn't thinking."

"No, *tesorino*, you weren't."

He rolled to his back, threw one arm over his head and stared at the ceiling. I had to make this right.

"I'm sorry," I started. "I didn't think about the shower in the basement. I figured that was...I don't know, you helping a scared victim you had rescued."

"You figured wrong. I don't make it a habit of showering with women. We already discussed the victim statement. I apologized for that. We gonna rehash that, too?"

Whoa. I knew I'd screwed up, but he was over-the-top mad.

"I'm trying to apologize here. I've spent the last few weeks locked in a room, having to pee a few feet from where I slept, I was woken up every morning by being kicked in the stomach. I was told repeatedly I was going to die. Then I get rescued only to find out my father's not dead, but the Attorney General of the United States and someone kidnapped me because he has someone they want back. Oh, and now that person wants to kill me if my new daddy doesn't deliver." I was on a roll, I might as well let it all hang out. I closed my eyes and rushed the rest out. "Then I go on the run with a man that is by and far the hottest man I've ever laid eyes on. Only he doesn't like to speak to me. Which honestly worked out well considering the moment I saw him I felt an instant unexplainable and probably unhealthy attachment to him. I'm sorry I am not thinking clearly. I don't think you're that kind of man. Frankly, I didn't believe you were...you know...in the shower. I thought you were testing me to see if I would try something with you even though I knew you had a woman."

I braved opening my eyes and was shocked to see Leo's smug grin.

"So, when you saw me get out of the shower with my cock hard enough to hammer nails, you thought what? I always sport wood?" Leo laughed.

Jerk.

"After everything I said, you want to discuss your... thing?" I huffed.

"Well given the opportunity, yeah, I'd like to address my cock first. Though I don't think it's ever been called a *thing* before."

"I wasn't thinking about why your cock was hard, you ass. I was too in shock at the size of it. Honestly, my first thought was you had to be a virgin because there is no way that it would fit in a woman."

"Oh baby, I can assure it'll fit, nice and snug and make you scream. And please don't say the word cock again," he groaned.

"Why not, you call it that?"

"Because hearing you say *cock* makes me want to fuck you, and we have things to talk about first."

He wanted to fuck me? I didn't think he even liked me. Not that *that* always mattered for a guy, but I figured it did for Leo.

"First, I'm a man, not a boy. I don't need to test you, nor would I ever. I showered with you because the second I met you I felt a protectiveness I have never felt wash over me. Not with my sister and not with my ma. Which scared me shitless. I'm an Italian American, and we are notorious for being mama's boys. I love my ma. That brings me to why I was silent. I was trying my hardest not to get close to you. I thought it was better if I kept my distance because I have an irrational draw to you. And it's not only physical. Though, I won't lie that is part of it. When I buckled your seatbelt in Maryland and your nipples puckered when my arm brushed against you, I wanted to lay you out on the hood of my truck and take you right then and there. What scares me is the emotional attachment I feel. I've dated women for months and not felt an ounce for them what I feel for you, a woman I know very little about. For a man like me, that's enough to make me crazy." Sweet baby Jesus he felt the same way I did. Only he wasn't smiling anymore. I felt a *but* coming. "There is one more reason I kept my distance. You're twenty-five and still wet behind the ears. I've been places and done bad things – I still do them. I'm fucked up, I have enough boxes nailed up tight to fill a cargo ship. And I don't do slow. I have one speed when I want something: Mach one and full steam ahead. That's who I am, and there's no use pretending I'm not."

I didn't appreciate the wet behind the ears statement, but I could work with all the rest.

"How old are you?" I asked.

"Thirty-two."

"How many siblings?"

Leo smiled catching on to what I was doing.

"Marco, he's a cop; Luca, he works in IT; and Arabella."

"I'm an only child. Er...I think. How many tours did you do?"

His smile faded. Now we were getting into personal territory. I waited a few seconds and when he still hadn't answered I decided to give him some of my truths.

"I graduated the University of Maryland at twenty-one. I was a good, straight-laced student. I started Georgetown Law studying constitutional law. I hated every minute of it. I thought I was doing what was expected of me. Following in my mother's footsteps, making her proud." I blew out a breath and prepared myself for his judgment. "I lost my virginity while at UM, I was twenty-one. It was with a frat boy. I just wanted to cash in my V-card. I wasn't forced, and it wasn't unpleasant, though it wasn't satisfying either. It was merely, okay. I had no real want to have sex again, so I didn't, until about nine months ago. I woke up one day and realized how much I hated my life. After that thought, I felt like a guilty asshole. I'd graduated from a top university, and it was paid for. I was in law school, again it was being paid for. I had a nice apartment, all paid for. Yet, I hated every part of it.

"I started going out more and studying less. My grades slipped, and when they did, I didn't care. I only wanted to have fun. I had sex with more guys than I can remember. Most of them drunken one-night stands. About three months before I was taken, I woke up in a stranger's bed and was disgusted with myself that I didn't know his name. I stopped sleeping around but didn't stop partying. The night I was taken, I was at a club drunk. A man was flirting with me at the bar, bought me a drink. After I drank it, I started to feel sick. I went to the bathroom, and the last thing I remembered was him catching me before I passed out. Me being kidnapped? That was my fault. I was alone and drunk. I'll have to live with the knowledge that my stupidity almost got me killed."

"I went through BUD/s when I was eighteen. After graduation, I was assigned to Group ONE Team Three in Coronado. After I finished that six-year enlistment contract, I reenlisted and transferred to Group TWO Team Eight. I finished my career with the Eightballers. I've been on more tours than I want to remember. I decided not to reenlist when my second contract came up because my second to last tour I had to kill three ten-year-old kids. After that, I was done. Having to put a bullet in a kid's forehead fundamentally changes a man. And the change was not that I felt remorse over having to kill a child, it was because I had none. Pulling the trigger that time felt no different than any other time. That's when I knew I was done."

"What was BUD/s like?"

I had watched the documentaries on cable, had even met a few SEALs while visiting my mom or Mr. Anderson at the White House. However, I had never actually known one.

"Unexplainable. Every day the instructors beat you down physically and mentally to see how far you can go before you ring out. And every time the bell is rung signaling another man has quit makes your ass pucker thinking you're next. And anyone who tells you differently is either full of shit or wasn't really there. There is not a man who has completed Basic Underwater Demolition SEAL school that didn't at one-point question why he was there and ringing the bell for the beer the instructor promised. That is the point of mentally beating you down, to see if you'll break. When every single part of you hurts and you don't think you can push on, what then? The movies and TV shows will tell you that SEALs are physically the strongest men in the military. That's good drama but not true. My height and weight hindered me. It was the shorter, lean guys who had less trouble on the run and swim quals. SEALs are *mentally* tough. We are trained to think around a problem. We don't shove a square peg into a round hole with brute strength we figure out, on the fly, how to make our peg round."

I had never thought about the mental aspect of being a SEAL. The movies show them all as supermen, with super-human abilities. None of them mention that they are really MacGyver's on steroids.

"Do you miss being a SEAL?"

"I am a SEAL. There is no such thing as an ex-SEAL. Do I miss active duty? No. I think I do more good now than I ever did while enlisted."

"When you learn to trust me, will you ever talk to me about your cargo ship of boxes?" That was the question that was weighing on my mind.

We had both admitted we were attracted to each other. I wasn't naive enough to think we'd get married or anything, but I was interested in seeing where this could go, at whatever speed he wanted to go. However, I knew myself well enough to know I could never be with someone that shut me out of the important parts of their life.

"I do trust you, but probably not. Some things are better left put away. You know more about me than any woman I have ever been with. Hell, my brothers don't even know the story about why I left the Navy."

"I asked if you would talk to me about your boxes, not let me help you unpack them. Those boxes are yours. If you need to keep them stacked in the corner, I'll make room in my closet. What I don't want is to have to navigate around them. Without knowing where they are, I will inadvertently knock one over. I get why you keep things locked up. I won't push the issue."

As the seconds ticked on, my heart sank. I thought I'd pushed too far and lost him. As much as I wanted to get to know Leo better, to use his words, this was non-negotiable for me.

"Okay, *tesorino*. But on my time," he conceded.

He agreed. I couldn't believe he actually said okay. My heart pounded in my chest and butterflies fluttered in my belly.

What now?

15

LEO

Something had woken me up. I didn't hear anything except Olivia's soft exhale on my chest. Call it a sixth-sense or years on the battlefield. Something wasn't right. I had left the closet light on when we went to bed. I could still see the light under the door, so I knew the power had not been cut. I slowly rolled Olivia to her side and sent Z a quick text.

I tagged my pants off the floor and slid my feet into my boots. I pulled back the blinds in the bedroom just enough to check the front of the house, nothing. As I let the blinds gently fall back into place my phone vibrated in my pocket.

Zane had alerted the team, and they were on standby.

"Olivia," I whispered, "wake up." I waited for her

eyes to open. "I need you to get up and get in the closet. All the way to the back."

I really wished she knew how to shoot. It was too dangerous to give her a weapon without her knowing what to do.

Olivia didn't ask questions as she got up and quietly made her way into the closet. Right before she stepped in I pulled her back and softly kissed her lips. I couldn't wait another second. It wasn't a long passionate kiss, it was a light touch of our lips. The type of kiss a man gives the woman he loves before he gets out of bed in the morning.

I was so damn proud of her when she slipped into the closet and shut the door behind her. I needed Olivia hidden away so I could search the house.

The living room was completely dark giving me enough freedom to move around and check the windows. I was at the back door when my pocket vibrated. I pulled my phone out and read Zane's text. What the fuck? Before I could reply, Zane, Jaxon, and Colin came through the front door, flipping the lights on as they entered. Each man had their guns leveled at Gomez and one of his men.

"You thought it was a good idea to bring him in the house?" I asked Zane. "You know I promised Abe we wouldn't get blood on his floors."

Gomez grunted at the same time Zane rolled his

eyes. He thought I was joking, I wasn't. I was ready to get this over with and take Olivia home.

"Where are the other two he came with?" I asked as Garrett joined the team.

"Abe and Wolf are currently having a chat with them at the bottom of the hill," Z told me.

Zane pushed the men farther into the room. At least their hands were zip-tied, but that still didn't mean shit. How did we know that Gomez didn't have a whole army of cartel members on standby?

"We're gonna have a little talk with Gomez before we dispose of him. He seems to think he has some information we want," Zane explained and guided Gomez to the kitchen table. "Have a seat."

Jaxon followed suit and shoved the man in front of him to the table.

"What information might that be?" I prompted.

We didn't have time to fuck around. Olivia was in the closet upstairs, and we had to move as quickly as possible.

"You have a traitor in your ranks," Gomez spoke.

Well, no shit Sherlock. We knew that, and we knew he knew that.

"You don't say?" I quipped.

"And you thought you needed to come all the way to the US to impart that wisdom on us?" Z asked.

"In Bolivia, men do business face to face. We do not cower behind a screen. I prefer to look a man in the eyes if he is going to threaten my life." Gomez sat back in his seat with a smug look crossing his face. This man had balls.

I walked around the table and pushed the muzzle of my Sig to his forehead. "How's this for looking you in the eyes. I'm going to put a bullet in your skull. You don't have shit to tell us."

"I did not take that pretty young girl. None of my men have been in the US for some time. You Americans are so stupid. If I had the girl, I would've killed her. I do not play games and take and release. There is no release. Never release, if I want to take, I do it. Then they die. You have a traitor. And not the idiot Clark who was merely a boy trying to keep up with men. You found him dead, yes?"

I was struggling to keep my cool. Though something he said struck me as the truth. Gomez's work up did show that he was ruthless. He always killed his enemies. He never even tortured them.

I glanced at Zane who seemed to be contemplating the same thing I was. Zane pulled his phone out, when he spoke to Gomez, he didn't lift his eyes from the screen. "Yes, and we got your note telling us he was a gift from you."

Gomez threw his head back and laughed. "Do I strike you as an altruist man? I do not give gifts." Gomez's demeanor changed when he looked up at me with fire in his eyes. "You think you are the only ones who have the capability to track information. I am here as a courtesy. I will tolerate the gun to my head for only so long before I take it as an insult. Siles is not who you think he is. He was planning a coup. Do you not think I knew that the sweep was fake? The American's only hit my smallest territories. If they had information about my operation, they would have gone to my largest warehouses. Siles is a traitor to me, an informant. I did not contact the Americans wanting him back. His men did."

"And we are supposed to believe you?" I asked.

If what Gomez was saying was true, Siles had outsmarted the Attorney General. Nothing like having the Americans take out the leader of the cartel so you could slide into his place. After we killed Gomez, Siles would no longer need to be in protective custody. He would be free to go back to Bolivia.

"Of course not. I know better than that. If you'll take your gun off my head and take my watch off, you'll find a chip in the back with all the information you need. Minus your traitor."

"What does that mean, minus our traitor?" If this motherfucker thought he was taking Olivia as a trade, I blow his head off, floors be damned.

"It simply means I didn't waste my time looking into your problem. Simple deduction tells me that someone is feeding Siles information and passing information back to Bolivia. I don't much care who it is. That is the American's problem. My time is worth money. If I cannot make money, I do not bother with it."

I lowered my gun and shoved it into the waistband of my jeans. I removed Gomez's gold diamond encrusted Rolex and had to force myself not to roll my eyes. How cliché. Once the back was off, the chip was removed, and I passed it to Garrett. He wasted no time slipping it into a reader and inserting it into his computer.

The room remained silent as Garrett's fingers flew across his keyboard.

"Should I play the audio?" Garrett asked.

Zane nodded and the room filled with Olivia's screams. What the fuck! I had zero interest in hearing Olivia being beaten.

"Please." Olivia's pleas could be heard in the background.

"It's almost time. The message has been sent. Leave the girl behind tomorrow and be far away when they come." A man's voice came on the recording.

"Yes, sir." A second man came on and acknowledged the order.

"Please, stop," Olivia screamed in the background.

"Awe, what a beautiful sound. Capo will go down fast once they find the girl, and all will work out." The first man was speaking again.

The recording stopped, and Garrett continued to type furiously on his keyboard.

"Voice confirmed," Garrett announced. "Jose Siles. The second man cannot be confirmed."

"Fuck," Zane exploded. "I really fucking hate when scumbags try to double-cross each other. Do you know the extra paperwork that goes with this shit?"

The vein in the side of Zane's neck was pulsing, a sure sign he was close to losing control.

"Where did you get that recording?" I asked Gomez.

"You don't think you're the only ones that have information dealers, do you?" Gomez smiled and looked at the man next to him.

"Timestamps authenticated matching the call logs from tango one to the Scotland address. Though the recording from the holding block has been deleted on their end," Garrett announced.

Gomez's information checked out. Siles did make a phone call. All prisoner calls are recorded, but miraculously the recordings from the prison had all been deleted. Isn't that special. Now we had to track who deleted those calls and who allowed a witness in protective custody to make a call. This was a clusterfuck.

"What do you want?" Zane asked Gomez.

"For you to get out of my business," he replied.

"That's it?" Zane inquired.

Something seemed off, it was too easy.

"And I have one small request. When you slice that motherfucker's throat, tell him I say hello."

"I can do that," Zane agreed. "And you won't mind if my men escort you back to the airport?"

"I thought we'd sightsee for a day or two." Gomez smiled.

"Not gonna happen. I'll have my plane on the tarmac in one hour to take you home." Zane was back on his phone tapping out a message.

"And we have a deal?" Gomez asked.

"We do."

I didn't wait for Gomez to be escorted out of the house. Instead, I took the stairs two at a time needing to get to Olivia as quickly as possible.

When I opened the closet door, she was huddled in the corner with a metal hanger in her hand waving it in front of her. I wasn't sure what she thought she was going to do with it, but she looked damn adorable doing it.

"Come out, *tesorino*. It's safe now." I reached my hand in to help her to her feet.

"Are you okay? I was so scared; you were taking so long." She catapulted her body into my arms and cried.

"I'm so proud of you for staying in here. I'm sorry it took so long. Everything is fine. We can go home soon." Every muscle in her body tightened. "What's wrong?"

"Nothing. I'm just happy you're okay," she whispered.

"You're happy so your body locked up? Tell me," I demanded.

I pulled back so I could look at her. Something was definitely wrong.

"I'm scared," she admitted.

"I told you, everything is fine now. We're okay to go home."

"That's not what I'm scared of."

I didn't understand. I thought she'd be happy to go home not scared. Maybe she didn't want to have to face the situation with her mom.

"Then what?" I asked.

"What happens when we get home? Now that you don't have to babysit me, will I see you again?"

"I was not babysitting you. I was protecting you, and happily."

"I'm afraid I'm going to lose you, and I just found you." I pulled her back, hugging her tight. "I can't lose you."

"I'm not going anywhere, *tesorino*. We'll figure it out." She sniffed a few times and wiped her nose on my tee. "You're mine, Olivia. I don't plan on letting you go. And I hope you're ready for me. If you're not or you need more time, you need to speak up now."

"I'm ready."

"For both our sakes, I hope you are."

There was no more denying that I was falling for this girl. This slip of a woman did what no one else had ever been able to do. She made me think about the future.

16

OLIVIA

I was exhausted. Leo and I never did go back to sleep after he came and got me out of the closet. Even though we could hear the guys downstairs talking, we stayed in bed and talked. I told him more about college and growing up. He told me about his family and what a pain in the ass his sister Arabella was. Though when he complained about her, he did it with a smile on his face. He adored his baby sister. His family sounded wonderful, and I hoped I'd get to meet them. His brothers sounded a lot like him, just not as badass. He wasn't joking when he said he was a mama's boy. I loved it. He told me about his father passing away when he was sixteen and how he and his brothers all stopped playing sports so they could take care of their mom and sister. At that moment, I knew I was falling in love with him. It was silly and too fast, and downright ludicrous. But it was happening.

Shortly after dawn Zane knocked on the bedroom door and told us the plane was ready to take us back to Maryland. I couldn't help that I was so nervous. I knew what Leo told me, he didn't want to let me go, but I was still scared. Even without the threat of a crazy man wanting to kill me, my life was still a mess. Most of which was my doing. I had to sort out school and figure out what I wanted to do with myself now that I had all but failed out of law school.

Then there was my mother. I didn't know where to begin with her and Peter. Was he still mad at her, too? Would he want to get to know me, or would he be too mad at my mom and not want anything to do with either of us. I wouldn't blame him if that was the case.

I guess what had me so worried was there was only so much crazy a man can deal with before he runs. I was afraid I was pushing the line.

All the way to the airport Leo kept his arm around me. He was constantly touching me in some way. Which did wonders to calm my nerves. When we boarded Zane's private jet, Leo walked us straight to the back and buckled us in. I figured he'd need to go and talk with his team, but he didn't leave my side. I told him I would be fine if he needed to work. He said that he would work later.

Shortly after takeoff, I rested my head on Leo's shoulder and fell asleep.

"Wake up, Olivia." I felt Leo's lips on my forehead, and I didn't want to open my eyes. I was too afraid it was a dream and he wasn't really there.

"How much longer?" I asked, keeping my eyes closed.

"We've landed," he chuckled. "You sleep like a rock."

"I do when you're close. I know I'm safe."

His lips stilled on my forehead, and he squeezed my hand. "You have no idea how much I like hearing that."

"It's the truth. I don't think I've ever in my life slept so soundly. Even when I knew someone was trying to kill me, the moment you got into bed with me and held me, I could sleep."

"Come on. We need to get off this plane before you say anything else sweet that will make me want to lay you across these seats and finally take you." Yes, please! I quickly tried to come up with something else to say. "Up you go, troublemaker. I can hear the wheels in your head turning."

"How'd you know?" I laughed.

"I saw the smoke coming out of your ears."

With a quick peck on my lips, he was standing. I wholeheartedly agreed, we had to get off the plane. That was the second time he had pressed his lips against mine and neither time had I gotten to taste him.

We got off the plane, and two SUVs were waiting on the tarmac for us.

"Your truck?" It dawned on me that we drove his truck to California, all the guys drove.

"Already being shipped back," he answered.

"Just like that?" What in the world? We could've driven it back to Maryland.

"Yep. Just like that."

He helped me into the front passenger side of one of the SUVs and buckled me in. Holy hell, this man takes seat belt safety seriously, he is constantly strapping me down. My mind wandered, and I wondered what it would be like to have him strap me down if I was naked.

"What was that thought?" he asked.

"Umm. I don't know? Why?"

"Your cheeks are pink, and you have the sexiest blush across the top of your cleavage. What were you just thinking about?"

"About how you take seat belt safety seriously and you like to strap me down," I admitted.

"You have no idea, *tesorino*. I hope to God you are ready for this. Give me five minutes with Zane, and we'll be on our way."

Leo shut the door and walked a few feet away from our car to where Zane was standing with Garrett and

Jaxon. I still hadn't asked where we were going or what was happening. I didn't want to know. I wanted to continue to live in my happy bubble where he would be with me every night to hold me. I didn't want to think about what was going to happen when he dropped me off at my apartment. He only lived forty minutes away from me, but right now that sounded like an eternity. I wished I had my cell phone, I wanted to text Caroline and tell her she had been right. I wondered if big badass navy SEALs liked cookies? I needed to send them something to thank them for helping me. I'd ask Caroline when I talked to her. I bet she'd tell me to send a fruit basket or something equally as healthy. None of the guys had an ounce of fat on them, I doubted they indulged in cookies.

Leo got into the car and started to pull away. I looked out the window, and Zane was staring at the car with what would be considered a smile for Zane. The man always looked grumpy, but one side of his mouth was tipped up. I waved goodbye, and his face broke out into a wide grin. Wow, he was hot when he actually smiled and didn't look like he was waiting to kill something.

"I called your mom and told her we were back in town and you were safe. I also told her I'd bring you by her place tomorrow to talk to her. She argued and wanted you tonight. I figured you needed another night to get your head straight before you saw her. I explained that to her, but she still wanted you tonight. So, I told her she no longer got to make demands on you. That I was making the decisions. Babe, I don't think your ma likes me."

There really wasn't anything funny about anything that Leo had just said, yet I couldn't stop myself from giggling. I could picture my mom blowing a gasket at Leo.

"I'm sorry. I could've called her."

"Yes, you could have. Two things. One I called her because selfishly I do not want you stressed out tonight. I want you all to myself without a bunch of crap swirling around in your head. Second, I don't want you stressed – ever. If I can ease the burden, I will. I made the call, it's done. Your ma is pissed at me. She'll figure out soon enough what you mean to me, and where we're headed, and I assume she'll get over it."

There was so much he'd just said that made me want to burst into tears. I had never had anyone want to ease the burden for me. It was always me and my mom. She worked hard and long hours and had her own stress to deal with. Don't get me wrong, she was a good mom. She provided for me, and I knew she loved me. But, she never had much time for me. Before she was Mrs. Anderson's White House aide, she had worked for a senator and had even less time for me.

"Thank you."

"Are you hungry?" he asked.

"Starving."

I was happy to report I had my appetite back, and I was making up for lost time. I couldn't stop eating. I still had to take antibiotics for the infection, but my wrist felt better. I was no longer keeping it covered. The red open sores had scabbed over, and it was healing. At first, I was worried about it leaving a scar. But now, I wouldn't mind if it did. I would use the scar as a reminder of what I had lived through.

We left the airport lot, but instead of heading toward the Beltway into DC, Leo followed the signs to Annapolis. I really wanted to ask Leo what happened while I was in the closet, who was downstairs, and how they worked everything out. But I knew he wouldn't tell me, and somehow, I knew he'd be disappointed in me if I asked. I trusted him. If he said it was safe to come home, then it was. I didn't need to know the details.

Leo seemed lost in his thoughts as he maneuvered us through traffic. Sitting in silence with him now seemed different than the times before. It was comfortable instead of nerve-wracking. And it gave me a chance to study his features while he was relaxed. His strong grip on the steering wheel, his eyes constantly checking the mirrors scanning the traffic all around us. What I wouldn't give to have that watchful stare focused on me. Those rough hands touching every inch of my body. I squeezed my thighs together to relieve some of the ache my thoughts provoked.

He was downright sexy. There were no two ways about it.

"*Tesorino*, you need to stop thinking whatever it is you're thinking about," Leo broke the silence.

I watched as he expertly crossed over three lanes of traffic to merge onto the exit ramp. "What are you talking about?"

"I'm talking about the blush on your face and how you pressed your legs together. Your body cannot hide your thoughts. I am holding on by a thread. A very weak, frayed thread."

Busted!

Perceptive bastard.

I didn't bother making excuses, he knew exactly what I was thinking. I suppose I should've been embarrassed, him knowing how badly I wanted him. But I wasn't. I liked it.

We pulled into an upscale neighborhood on the outskirts of Annapolis. The houses were older but very well kept. Leo pulled into a driveway and cut the engine.

"If at any time you get overwhelmed or you've had enough, squeeze my hand three times and I'll make our excuse to leave." Leo took the keys out of the ignition and grabbed his phone out of the cup holder and exited the car. Leaving me sitting in the car wondering where we were and why I'd be overwhelmed. He opened my door and helped me down. The moment I was situated on his left side, he put his arm around my waist and pulled me tight.

I loved it.

Absolutely loved when he touched me.

Leo didn't bother knocking when we got to the door, nor did he unlock it. We walked right in. The first thing that hit me was the smell. Garlic and the sweet smell of basil. It was heavenly. The next thing that registered was the loud laughter. I looked around the room. It wasn't huge, nor was it small. It was the perfect size to gather a family around and watch TV or play a board game on the large coffee table that sat in front of the well-worn sectional couch. This was a family home. There were photographs on every available surface. School pictures, military basic training photos, police academy graduation pictures – family pictures. This was so different than the sterile apartment in DC I had grown up in. There were no family memorabilia hanging on our walls. Hell, there was no family. Just me and my mom.

It finally hit me where I was. Leo's ma's house.

My frantic eyes looked up at Leo. "You'll be fine, *tesorino*. Promise."

He lowered his face, and his lips found mine. This time I wasn't letting him pull back before I could finally taste him. I licked the seam of his lips, and he opened his mouth. Finally! The first brush of his tongue against mine sent an electric shock wave through my body. He pulled back, kissing my bottom lip then stopped our kiss altogether to look at me.

"Did you feel that, *tesorino*?" Leo whispered.

"Yes."

"*Figlio*! You're home." I heard from across the room, breaking our moment.

I jumped back from Leo like we'd been caught doing something we shouldn't have been doing. Well, we had been and were caught by Leo's mom.

Leo chuckled and pulled me closer to him, not allowing me to run and hide. "Hi, Ma."

Leo's mom stood across the room staring at us. For a moment, I thought she was going to tell me to leave. Then her lips tipped, and her entire face lit up.

"Bella! Two more plates at the table." I could've sworn I heard her voice crack.

I looked back to Leo. "Did you tell them we were coming? I don't want to impose."

"There is no imposing on Sunday dinners, *tesorino*. Ma always makes more than enough," Leo explained.

"She's finally here." Leo's mom said softly from across the room.

"Ma," Leo warned, his voice strong but his face gentled when he looked at his mom.

"Don't *Ma* me. Now introduce me to your girl so I can take her and get to know her," his mom instructed.

Whoa, now I understood where Leo got his bossiness from.

"Olivia, this is my ma, Alessandra Gillonardo. Her friends call her Essa. Ma, Olivia Cox."

"It is a pleasure to meet you, Mrs. Gillonardo. Thank you for allowing me to stay for dinner. I hope it isn't any trouble."

Essa's brow lifted, and she studied me. "You call me Ma. And family is never an imposition, *ragazza dolce*. Come, let's go check on the kitchen. Bella has been in there too long by herself. You never know what that girl will do."

I was stuck in place, as panic washed over me. This fear was worse than knowing someone was trying to kill me. Leo's mom had demanded I go with her, alone. There was no invitation in her tone, she was not asking me to follow her. She was telling me I *was* to follow her. I had never done this before. The whole meet the parents thing. Leo loved his mom. What if she hated me and I screwed this all up?

"You'll be fine. She's going to love you," Leo whispered into my hair.

Essa was standing across the room waiting for me to follow her. She wasn't going to take no for an answer.

Time to pull up my big girl panties and meet the family.

I woodenly followed Essa into the kitchen. A

slender girl with long wavy dark hair was bent over a cutting board chopping more garlic.

"No more garlic, *Figlia*. You'll give everyone the sweats," Essa told the girl.

I was going to have to pick up a handy-dandy English to Italian pocket dictionary. I knew more French than Italian. So far, I was able to keep up with Essa. She called the girl, figlia – daughter. This had to be Arabella.

"Ma, it needs more." Arabella stopped chopping to look at her mom and noticed me. "Who's this?" she asked.

"Your brother's wife," Essa answered.

I nearly choked on my tongue.

Wife!

"Mrs. Gillonardo, we're not married," I sputtered. What on earth gave her the idea we were married?

"Ma, you call me, Ma, like all of my other children," Essa corrected. "Something you need to understand, I did not raise my boy to be a boyfriend. I raised him to be a husband. Do you understand?"

"No," I admitted.

I had no idea what Essa was talking about, and frankly, she was freaking me out.

"I mean, my son has never brought a woman to meet me. And certainly, would never think to sit a woman at my table that he didn't indeed to keep. He is a husband. I have been waiting for you, *Figlia*. Waiting for my son to bring me his wife. You are one more piece that will complete this family. Gillonardo men, they are strong and stubborn, and you will have to learn to stand up to him and when to concede. My boys are their father's sons; when they find the woman who was made for them, they will never let that woman go."

"I don't know if I'm that to him," I admitted. All of what Essa said? I wanted that. I wanted to be the woman that was made for Leo. "He only met me a few days ago. I think he brought me here because he missed you."

"Do you love my son?"

Holy shit. I was having the "Do you love my son" talk with Leo's mom ten minutes after meeting her.

"Yes," I whispered. Realization dawned that I wasn't *falling* in love with him. I was *in* love with him, and the thought of not being with him would leave a gaping hole in my soul that would never go away.

"Good. I married my Marco two weeks after we met. He wouldn't take no for an answer. I tried to fight and play hard to get. But it was no use. When a Gillonardo man wants something he..."

I cut her off and finished her sentence. "Has one speed. Full steam ahead." I repeated what Leo had told me.

"Ah, yes, you already know." Essa laughed. "Good, I see my boy has prepared you. Welcome to the family, my darling girl. I am pleased my son has chosen well. Though, Gillonardo men, they have impeccable taste in women. There was never doubt you wouldn't be perfect."

I wasn't sure what I was supposed to say to her. Everything was happening so fast. I still had my doubts as to what was going on between me and Leo. The fairy tale that Essa spoke of sounded like wishful thinking of a mom that loved her son and wanted him to be happy.

I noticed that Arabella was no longer looking at me but over my shoulder. I turned my head to see what had caught her attention and three men stood behind me. They could've been triplets. All three were tall, but Leo was an inch at most taller than the other two. They all had the same olive skin and dark hair with matching green eyes. But it was Leo I couldn't take my eyes off of. I wasn't sure if he was mad at me, or his mom, or both of us. I didn't know how much of the conversation he had heard, but by the look on his face, it had been a lot.

Well damn. Now, what did I do?

"Now that Ma has scared you shitless, do I need to take you in the other room for a minute before you run? Or would you like to meet my brothers?" Leo asked.

"I'm not going to run," I assured him.

"Good. So, you're still ready?" he asked.

Were we really having this conversation in front of his whole family? His sister hadn't said a word to me and both his brothers were looking at me like a zoo animal on exhibit. What if they didn't like me? What if they thought I wasn't good enough to be a part of their family? They were very obviously close, more than close if Leo wanted to discuss our fledgling relationship in front of them. I thought back to what Leo said about my mom not liking him. He told me that once she saw what I meant to him, she'd get over it. That had to work both ways. If his siblings didn't welcome me the same way Essa had, they'd have to get over it. I would prove to them how much Leo meant to me.

"I have never been more ready in my life." I blew out a breath and squared my shoulders. "Introduce me to your brothers." I tried to keep my voice firm to not give away my nervousness.

"I like her, Brother," one of the men said and laughed.

"Come here, *tesorino*," Leo commanded.

He didn't have to ask me twice. I needed to feel his arms around me to settle the riot of emotions bouncing in my tummy.

"Olivia, this is my older brother, Marco Jr., we call him MJ." Leo pointed to his brother. "And this is Luca, my younger brother. I assume Ma already introduced you to Bella."

She had, but she hadn't. I didn't get to actually talk to Bella before we dove right into marriage and family.

"Hi everyone. It's nice to meet you all." I didn't know what else to say. I felt like I was on display and my every word was being scrutinized. I felt the need to flee from the men's watchful stare. The safest place for me was back in the kitchen. "What can I help with?" I asked Essa.

"Don't let them scare you, *Figlia*. Boys, stop staring at your brother's girl.

"Sorry, Ma. It's not every day I walk into the kitchen and find a beautiful woman standing there," Luca said.

"You better watch your mouth, Luca, Leo might kick your ass for looking at his girl." MJ laughed.

"He could try," Luca returned.

"I could try and not break Ma's furniture when I put my foot up your ass. Take your eyes off my woman," Leo growled.

Yes, he growled, like the jungle cat he so closely resembled.

"Language," Essa chastised. "If you boys are going to fight, go outside. My carpets were cleaned last week, and I hate having to blot the blood out of the carpet. I cannot wait until you three have sons and you know what it's like to referee unruly boys." Essa turned to me. "Only have girls. No sons. They may love their ma, but they are a pain in the ass."

I laughed at her use of a curse word so shortly after

she had corrected her sons. She might've called them a pain, but the love Essa had for her family was unparalleled.

"Would you all please not scare Olivia away before I get to talk to her? My whole life I wanted a sister, and now my dumb brothers are gonna scare you off before I get to keep you," Arabella spoke for the first time.

I didn't know if the butterflies in my belly were because I was freaked out that Essa and Bella said they wanted to keep me, or if it was from the excitement that they wanted to.

"Don't let her fool you. She acts sweet and innocent, but she is trouble. She'll rope you into her crazy schemes if you're not careful," MJ said.

"Shut up, MJ. I am not."

"Right." He smiled at Bella.

"Ma!" Bella whined.

"Sorry, *Figlia*, he is not wrong."

My head bounced around as they continued to bicker with one another. My gaze landed on Leo. He was leaning against the wall, his arms crossed over his chest watching me with his family. Peace washed over me. This was where I belonged. There was no doubt in my mind. Essa said I was made for him and they had been waiting for me. The truth was, they all were made for me, and I had been waiting for them.

17

LEO

I spent the night watching Olivia charm my family. She did nothing special, she didn't need to. My family had fallen in love with her just as fast as I had. There was something about her that was captivating. That should've scared the fuck out of me, but it didn't. I'd been around the block enough times to know that what I felt for Olivia was different. It was real. If there had been any sliver of doubt, it disappeared the second her soft tongue grazed mine. The current that sparked between us bonded me to her in a way that was unbreakable. It was like our souls had melted together.

My whole life Ma told me and my brothers that we'd know when we met the woman that God had intended for us. Each of us thought she was full of shit and dismissed her. Luca and MJ would never believe me if I told them that I thought Ma was actually right. Olivia was proof. They'd have to feel it themselves.

After the week we'd had, family dinner was exactly what we both needed. It was what I needed. Every Sunday if I wasn't on an op, my ass was planted at Ma's table. It wasn't because that was what was expected, though it was. It was because I needed them. I was close to every member of my team, they were my second family. We fought together, we bled together. I was bonded to them in a way that very few people could understand. However, my family grounded me, reminded me that I was more than a hired assassin sent in to kill bad guys so the government could deny involvement. Dinners around Ma's table reminded me why I do what I do – so they could be safe. I would take the hash marks on my soul if it meant my brothers, sister, and Ma could breathe easy and not have to know what evil looked like.

By the time we pulled up to my apartment Olivia looked dead on her feet. I felt a little guilty I had subjected her to all the ridonculous behavior. My brothers were the worst, telling her one wild story after another. She fit right in and laughed along with them, encouraging my siblings to tell her more. Arabella looked like she had a shiny new toy on Christmas morning, a sister she could play with. And Ma, I hadn't seen her so happy since before my dad died. Her family was getting bigger. She welcomed Olivia into the family without reservation. That did freak me out. I figured Ma would put Olivia through her paces. Instead, she cried and thanked me for bringing her a daughter. *Crazy woman.*

Now I was done fighting the pull between us. The mission objective had changed. I would do everything in my power to tie her to me. She repeatedly had told me she was ready. But the poor girl had no clue what full steam ahead really meant. She was about to find out, and I was willing to wear her down if she fought it.

This was it.

I pulled into the underground parking and parked. I was suddenly nervous, a wholly new feeling for me. I didn't get nervous – not on a mission, not with a woman, never.

"Everything alright?" Olivia asked, when I didn't get out of the car right away.

"Perfect," I answered.

"Then why are you staring out the windshield into space? Have you changed your mind?" she whispered the last part.

"Fuck no," I said a little more abruptly than I had intended. "Truth? And I can't believe I'm telling you this, only further hammering home how I feel about you. This is new for me. I'm scared that all of this will be too much for you and you'll run. I'll chase you down if you do, but I'm not used to this feeling. Hell, I'm not used to feeling at all."

"You won't have to chase me. I won't run."

She says that now. But she is twenty-five and has her whole life in front of her. She could have a man without a cargo ship full of guilt and memories. She could have a man that is not scarred on both the outside and inside.

"Do you want to know what I was thinking when I was sitting in your mom's house? How good it felt to be there. How much I loved them already. That I hoped they would accept me because if they didn't, and I lost you, I would never recover. And I thought your mom was wrong. I was not made for you. Leo, you were made for me. Not to save me from bad guys, but to save me from a lonely, loveless life. Because if you hadn't come into my life, that's what it would've been – a half-life.

With a few words, this woman soothed my fears.

"One last thing. You know what I do for a living. You know that most of my ops are top secret. I cannot tell you about them, or where I'm going. Most of the time I won't know for how long. When I leave for work, you have to know I go out with the intention of killing someone. I've never thought what my job would mean to someone else because I've never considered bringing anyone else into my life."

I waited for her to fully comprehend what I did. When I said I was going hunting, I meant that literally.

Only I wasn't hunting cute, furry, defenseless animals. I was hunting the human variety of animals.

"Will you come straight home to me after you get back?" she asked.

I wasn't sure she was grasping what I was telling her. "Do you understand what I'm telling you?"

"Yes, Leo. I fully understand what your job entails. It has no bearing on how I feel about you. I'm proud of what you do. I don't need to know the details. In fact, it's better that I don't. I will not get in the way of your job, I'll stand next to you, and wait for you to come home. Now will you come straight home to me in DC or will I need to meet you in Annapolis?"

Silly girl. She thought she still lived in DC.

"Annapolis," I answered.

"Perfect. You call me when you land back in Baltimore, and I'll hightail my ass to see you. My insurance will probably skyrocket with all the speeding tickets I'm going to get. But I don't care."

She still wasn't getting it.

"Olivia, I want you here in Annapolis," I told her.

"And I will be. As soon as you call, I'll be right here. Promise." She smiled at me.

"No, *tesorino*. I want you in my apartment – permanently," I explained.

Her smile faded, and she cocked her head to the side. "I don't think I'm understanding."

"I want you to live here, with me."

"What? Are you crazy?" she asked.

Now she was getting it.

"I told you, full steam ahead. There's no use waiting. I know what I want."

"This isn't full steam ahead. This is breaking the speed of light, or sound, or whichever is faster. I can't move in."

She was fucking hot when she was flustered. I wished I'd waited to have this conversation in my apartment.

"Why not?" I asked.

"What if you don't like how I brush my teeth or how I spit the toothpaste in the sink, or how I fall asleep reading with the light on? Or what if I'm a slob and leave my girly shit in your bathroom. I have a lot of it you know. And I own a lot of shoes. What if you don't want my shoes taking up your closet?"

"Stop. I don't give the first fuck how you brush your teeth or how you spit. That's a lie, I care if you spit." He paused to smile at me. "Lucky for you I don't have much in my closet, so there's room for your shoes, and if there's not, you can use the second bedroom for a closet. Same for the bathroom. Hell, we'll buy a house to fit all your girly shit if we need to. And check this woman, you will never again fall asleep reading when I am home. After I'm done with you, you'll be too rung out to think about a book."

A sly smile playing on her lips gave way to a

hundred-megawatt smile that I never wanted to see directed at another man. It was a smile that made me want to hand her the world.

"Can we buy a house in Ma's neighborhood so I can be close to her when you're gone?" she asked.

"Upstairs, now," I demanded.

Olivia's smile faded. "What's wrong?"

"Not a damn thing. You have no idea how right everything is. I knew I should've waited to have this conversation somewhere where I could lay you out and devour you. *Tesorino*, whether you meant to or not, you just sealed your fate. There is no running, there is no stopping. My dad had his ring on my Ma's finger in two weeks, and you thought that was fast? You ain't seen nothing."

I rushed her out of the car and into the elevator. I didn't speak to her on the way to my apartment because I needed the time to get myself under control. I wanted tonight to last, I wanted to show her what her words meant to me. How she'd slipped into my life and tied me in knots.

I didn't bother showing her around her new home – there was no time. I pulled her through the living room into the master bedroom at a fast clip, slowing down only to shut and lock the bedroom door behind us. I pulled my Sig from my holster, checked the safety was on, and put it on the nightstand. First order of business after we got her settled in was to teach her how to shoot. It was a must. There would always be a gun on the nightstand. She would have no choice but to learn how to use it.

"Shower." One word was all I was capable of saying. My body was on fire. I had never needed to feel a woman as badly as I needed Olivia. This was different. I wasn't looking for just a sexual release; my body ached to feel her. For the first time, I craved the intimacy of the act. I wanted to lay myself bare in front of her. For better or for worse, I wanted to let her see every part of me. She deserved nothing less.

Olivia didn't answer and started to undress. I followed suit, pulling my tee over my head. My eyes never left Olivia's body. The more skin she revealed, the more my eyes hungrily ate her up. She was stunning. I felt like I was ten feet tall when her pretty brown eyes caught fire and her chest heaved with every intake of breath. I never thought that the simple act of undressing could be so erotic, the best kind of foreplay. I forced myself not to reach out and touch her. My hand shook with the need to rip the rest of her clothes off her body in an effort to hurry things along.

When we were both naked, I took her hand and walked us into the bathroom. Once the water was warm enough, I pulled her into the shower and gathered her in my arms. I cradled her face in my hands and brushed her cheeks with my thumbs. She was so small next to me. I bent down and brushed my lips against hers. "You are so beautiful, my *tesorino*." Finally, I kissed her the way I had wanted to for days. Our tongues glided in a dance that could only be described as triumphant. I consumed her, sucked the breath from her body and in exchange gave her mine. It was the single most intimate moment I had ever experienced. Not that it surprised me, it was Olivia.

When I finally pulled back, she was breathless and flushed. Perfect.

"Turn around and face the wall." I was so much taller than she was I needed to be behind her to touch all the places I wanted to. She did as I asked and my hands immediately cupped both of her breasts. Heavy, full, and so fucking soft in my hands. I squeezed them and plucked at her nipples until her ass was rubbing against my hard cock pressed at the small of her back. I dared not look down, the sight of my cock on her bare skin would make me explode. Her breathy sighs turned into desperate moans. She was there.

"Are you ready?" I whispered in her ear, flattening my tongue on the soft skin below her lobe and licking down to her sexy collarbone.

"Yes," she whined.

I slid my right hand down her flat stomach until I reached her neatly trimmed curls. Normally I like a closer shave, but the sexy landing strip she left gave me just enough hair to tug. Her deep throaty moan that followed told me she liked it, too. My hand found her wetness, and I couldn't wait any longer. A few hard circles around her clit before I pushed two fingers inside of her.

"Leo," she panted.

"I'll get you there," I promised.

I only hoped it was before I came all over her back. Her ass was grinding on my cock harder, faster. I doubled my efforts and stroked the top wall of her pussy and pinched her nipple with my left hand.

She came on my hand with a low sexy whine calling my name over and over. I removed my fingers and shut off the water, uncaring that neither of us had actually washed. I needed a bed and her wrapped around my cock.

Fuck drying off, I didn't care that we were both soaking wet when I laid her on the bed and crawled over her.

"I don't want anything between us," I told her. "I'm clean, we're tested every month at work. I haven't been with a woman since my last test."

Olivia looked up at me, some of the fog clearing from her eyes. "I'm clean. Promise. I was tested after...you know."

"Baby, I wasn't telling you that because I don't trust you. I was more asking you if you were okay with us not using a condom."

"I'm not on birth control," she said with disappointment in her voice.

No birth control, I didn't need to think about what the ramifications of my next words meant. I knew what I wanted. I felt my heart pound in my chest, and suddenly everything clicked into place.

"I'm good with that. But, *tesorino*, if you're not, I'll grab a condom."

Unmoving, I waited for her to answer. Too afraid that if I even flinched my unruly cock would find her awaiting heat and it'd be too late for discussions. I wouldn't take this choice from her.

"I am, too." She smiled.

I reached between us and palmed my cock, rubbing the head against her clit. "You're sure? A hundred percent. I'm not going to pull out. You're okay if we make a baby?"

Never in any realm of my imagination did I think I would ever be having this conversation with a woman. I double and triple checked the condom every time I had sex. Hell, I would never even use a condom that a woman tried to supply.

My cock was throbbing with anticipation when she finally answered, "I'm okay with making a baby. Now please fuck me, Leo, I'm going to die if you don't," she begged.

I lined my cock up with her entrance and pushed the tip in, wetting it and pulling back. She was tight, I'd have to work my way in slowly or I'd hurt both of us.

I was a little more than halfway in when she started

to thrust her hips up to meet mine. "I'm not going to fuck you, Olivia. I'm going to love you," I whispered and slid home.

I stayed planted inside of her, rocking my hips, making sure to grind her clit with my movements. When her moans turned into sobs, I knew I needed to hurry this along.

"Lock your ankles behind my back and put your hands above your head. Hold on tight, baby."

She did as I asked providing me with the leverage I needed. I gathered both her hands in one of mine above her head and went to work giving her long hard thrusts.

My eyes rolled in the back of my head with the first spasm of her pussy. Once her orgasm broke and she tightened around my cock, heat rushed up my spine and my balls tingled. With one last hard thrust, I stayed planted and let myself go. The pleasure was unbearable, there was no stopping the moan that tore from my chest and my toes curling as I spilled into her. No barrier, nothing between us.

Nothing had ever felt sweeter.

18

OLIVIA

Nothing could bring me down. My head was bopping to the song playing in my mind on repeat, *...walking on sunshine, oh-oh...* I couldn't ever remember a better morning than this. Leo was absolutely right. After last night, the last thing that was on my mind was a book. After he got us up and dried us off, he ripped the wet comforter off the bed, and we slept tangled together like a pair of baby kittens. Full contact sleeping, that's what it was.

Not a single nightmare.

He got up and made us breakfast then excused himself to the extra bedroom which was set up as an office slash gym and said he needed to check in with Zane.

I made myself busy looking around his, I mean our, apartment. There wasn't much to look at really. It was definitely a bachelor pad, it was neat and tidy but lacking a woman's touch. That surprised me; I figured that Bella or Essa would've pushed their way in and decorated for him. He had a kickass balcony off his dining area with a great view of the water.

Leo came up from behind and wrapped his arms around me. "How are you feeling today?" he asked.

My face heated at his question remembering last night. "I'm a little sore," I admitted.

"Good, I like knowing you'll have a constant reminder of me all day." He kissed the side of my neck, heating other parts of my body. I pushed my ass back, happy to see I wasn't the only one affected by the memory.

"Oh no, wildcat. We need to talk first."

"Okay." I sighed.

I really didn't want to talk. I wanted to climb back into bed with him for the day and forget everything around us.

"Your ma is on the way over here. I thought it better than us going to her. With beltway traffic this time of day, I'd say we have an hour and thirty minutes." That snapped me out of my good mood. "We also need to sort your apartment in DC. I can have movers over there tomorrow, or if you want to go and pack, we can do it when I get back."

"Get back? What do you mean?"

"I have to leave tonight on an op. It should be

quick, a few days, tops. I would like for you to stay here. But you have a few options, Tom said you could stay at the White House in the personal residence. You could always stay with Ma or, and I can't believe I am suggesting this, Bella can come and keep you company here. But I swear to all things holy if she pulls her crazy shenanigans with you, I'll turn her over my knee."

"You wouldn't spank your sister." I laughed at the thought of big, tough Leo bending his adult sister over his knee.

"You have no idea what I'd do when it comes to you. God knows I love my sister, but she's a menace to society and needs to be leashed."

"No, she doesn't, and that's mean. She's perfectly fine. I could always go to my place and start packing."

If I went back to DC that would give me something to do. I wouldn't sit around and worry about what Leo was doing. Okay, that was a lie, I would still wonder, but at least I'd be busy.

"No, *tesorino*. I want you close to my team while I'm out of town."

I waited to see if he'd offer any further explanation. When he didn't, I studied his face and saw it left no room for argument. This had to be one of those times Essa was talking about when I had to make a choice to stand up to him or concede. Me staying here obviously was important to him, and really, his request didn't bother me.

"Okay."

There was no reason to make a stand when honestly, I didn't care. I would find something to do around here.

"Thank you. I pulled some house listings around Ma's neighborhood. You could go by yourself or take her. Whatever you want to do. Pick one, or don't. If there's nothing you like, we'll keep looking." Had he lost his mind? Buy a house, now? "Full steam, *tesorino*. There is no point of you moving in here, getting comfortable only to turn and move when we find out you're pregnant."

"Pregnant?" I spit out. Now I knew he had lost his mind. No, if's, and's, or but's. I had hooked my star to a crazy man.

"Oh yeah. I knocked you up last night. I felt it. There's no way I didn't."

He was serious. He thought I was pregnant.

"You *felt* it? You know you sound crazy, right?" I laughed.

"Well baby, if I didn't last night, I'm going to right now."

He pulled me off the couch and led me to the bedroom. He didn't waste any time divesting us of our clothes and tossing me on the bed. He was over me in a flash, and his lips were on mine. I loved kissing him.

He was gentle yet demanding. He sucked my tongue into his mouth giving me no choice but to submit. After he thoroughly pillaged my mouth, he leisurely pushed inside of me. Unlike me, he wasn't in a hurry.

"Please," I begged. The burn of him stretching me set the rest of my body on fire. He awoke every nerve ending. I brought my hips up trying to hurry him.

"Don't move. I don't want to hurt you."

I didn't care if it hurt; I wanted him now. I planted my foot on the bed and pushed with all my might to get him to his back. I knew it only worked because he didn't want to crush me under his weight.

Before he could chastise me for my stunt, I slammed down on him, taking him fully inside of me.

I screamed out, a mixture of pain and intense pleasure.

"Dammit, Olivia." Leo grabbed my hips and held me in place.

"I'm fine," I panted and tried to move, but he held me in place. I needed to move. I felt stuffed full, and the pain only intensified my desire.

"You damn near split yourself in half." His grip loosened, allowing me to lift a little before I slid back down. Leo groaned, and his fingers dug into my side, but he didn't stop my movements. "*Tesorino*, you have exactly two minutes to get yourself off riding my cock before I flip you back over."

My hips rocked back on every downward stroke. I

was holding out as long as I could, enjoying the look of rapture on his face. He was enjoying this as much as I was. I was so close yet willing myself not to let go. I knew the moment I came he'd take over.

"Sweet girl, I know what you're doing." Leo bucked his hips, sending shock waves through my body. If he moved this was all over, and I would come. "As much as I'm enjoying watching your tits sway as your tight pussy hugs my cock, you're done playing." He pushed up and held me in place rocking me back and forth. It was no use; I couldn't hold on any longer. "Come for me, Olivia."

My orgasm hadn't stopped pulsing through my body before he flipped us back over. "Now I'm going to make you scream. Hold on tight."

And he did. He made me scream not once but three times. By the time he pulled the last orgasm out of me, I was begging for him to stop. He did only after I promised never to hurt myself again. I promised, but we both knew it was a lie.

After we were done, he gathered me in his arms and kissed the top of my head. "We better get cleaned up, your ma is gonna be here soon."

"Way to harsh my mellow, Leo."

Leo's body was shaking with laughter under me. "Sorry, *tesorino*. I didn't think you wanted your ma to find us sprawled out in bed together."

"No. You're right. I'm gonna jump in the shower."

Leo started to get up with me. "Oh no, big boy, you stay here. If you get in the shower with me, I'll be walking bow-legged by the time my mom gets here."

Leo grabbed my hand and gave it a tug pulling my back to him. "You know I love you, right?"

He loved me. He said it. Leo *Panther* Gillonardo said he loved me. My heart jumped in my chest and thudded so hard I was sure Leo could hear it.

"You know I love you, too, right?" I smiled down at him.

"With every fiber of my soul, *tesorino*."

Sweet baby Jesus, I loved this man.

My heart was pounding again, only this time it was because my mom and Peter Newton had buzzed from the lobby announcing their arrival.

I was trying my hardest to play cool, but I was mad, and happy, and scared, and thought I might throw up.

Maybe Leo had knocked me up. Was it too early for morning sickness twelve hours after the seed was planted, so to speak?

The knock at the door made me jump. "Easy, Olivia. Everything will be fine."

Leo opened the door. There was my mom. Peter Newton stood beside her looking as nervous as I felt. Behind them, two agents stood guard. I wonder if there was still a threat on the Attorney General's life. I looked to Leo to ask.

"Protocol, *tesorino*. Everything is fine," he assured me.

Well, he tried to anyway. I didn't think anything would be okay again between me and my mom.

"Sweetheart," my mom cried and came to me. "I was so worried about you. Are you okay? Where did you go? You can come home now. We'll move you back into the penthouse for a while until you're all settled. We can leave now."

"That's enough, Pamela," Peter said from across the room.

Well, they hadn't worked anything out if the tone in Peter's voice was any indication.

"Back off," Leo demanded. "Slow down and give her a chance to talk."

This was not starting off well. My mother could get herself all worked up and would boss everyone in the room if not kept in check. That wasn't going to work with Leo. He would trample over her without thinking twice. Knowing he had my back gave me the courage I needed to face my mom.

"Why don't we sit down and talk," I suggested.

"We can do that in the car. Let's get your things and get out of Mr… Sorry, I forgot your name," my mom sneered.

Damn, she could be a bitch when she wanted to be.

"Not gonna happen. And you know damn well what my name is," Leo said.

"This is none of your business. It's a private family matter. You did your part. Now I'm taking my daughter home so we can speak in private." My mom squared her shoulders and prepared for battle.

"Not gonna happen, Pamela," Leo semi repeated.

"And just who do you think you are? I'm going to call..."

Leo cut her off. "I'm the man who is going to marry your daughter. And being that man, I'm going to make sure that while the three of you have your talk, Olivia is not overly upset. At any time during this conversation, if I feel like Olivia has had enough, I will shut this shit down so fast your head will spin. I understand this is an unfortunate situation and emotions are high, so I'll give you a little leeway. But I'll warn you, you're almost at the end of your rope. I get you don't like me, for reasons only known to you. And I'm okay with that. One day you'll come to appreciate that I'm telling you this to help you fix what you broke with your daughter: Back off and listen to her."

My mom huffed and started to say something else. Something that was undoubtedly rude and would make Leo toss her ass out.

"Sit down, Pamela, and let Olivia speak," Peter said from across the room.

Surprisingly, my mom did just that. She sat on the

couch, Peter next to her. I sat in the recliner, and Leo perched on the armrest. He never left my side. Not when I screamed at my mom for lying to me, not when she yelled back and told me I wasn't allowed to talk to her like that. Not for the entire hour when she deflected and refused to answer my questions. There was something wrong, my mom had never behaved in such a rude, belligerent manner before. The woman sitting in front of me was not the mom that raised me. I was done. She didn't want to talk to me; she only wanted me to side with her that everything that had happened was Peter's fault. Forget that she'd lied to both of us my whole life. One excuse after another. She was completely irrational.

"We're done here," Leo announced.

"What? No, we're not. Olivia still needs to pack," my mom said.

"I see you haven't been listening to a fucking word your daughter has said," Leo spat.

"Such vulgarity. And you think I'm okay with my daughter being with a man like you?"

"That's what you pulled from my statement? Since you haven't been listening, I'm gonna lay it out for you." Oh shit, that didn't sound good. "I'm going to continue to urge Olivia to find a way to forgive you. Not for you but for her. I don't want her living with anger knotted in her belly. When she falls asleep in my arms at night, she's gonna do it with a smile on her face, knowing her world is perfect. You're welcome in that life, but only if you don't come through that door spitting venom. Peter, the same goes for you. I'll do my best to support Olivia in forging a relationship with you if that's what you both would like. Olivia lives here now. In case you missed the part where she explained she didn't want to return to Georgetown, I'm gonna reiterate that for you. When she figures out what it is she wants to do, she'll tell you. In the meantime, she'll be taking time for herself to heal and be happy."

"Thank you, Leo," Peter said.

"Why are you thanking him, Peter? Can't you see he is manipulating her and bossing her around? He won't even leave her side," my mom protested.

"That's what a man does, Pamela. You'd know that if you'd stop busting balls for five minutes and listen. Leo is protecting her; he won't let anyone near her who will hurt her," Peter calmly explained to my lunatic of a mother. I'd never seen her so unhinged before. What was wrong with her?

"My daughter doesn't need protecting from me, and especially not by the likes of *him*."

"Obviously he thinks she does. And I have to say, not only do I agree with him, I'm impressed with his self-control." Peter sat farther back on the couch, clearly uncomfortable in the direction this had gone.

"Get out of my house." I'd had enough. I stood up, and in the process pushed Leo off the armrest, forcing him to stand as well. "I've tried to be civil and ask you questions. You refused to answer. I tried to talk to you about school. You refused to listen. I tried to apologize for my behavior over the last year. You refused to hear that. Fine, you don't want to participate in an actual conversation with me. No problem. But don't you ever disrespect Leo. Not ever in our home, and never in front of me. I will pick him over you every day of the week and twice on Sunday.

"I know you tried your best while I was growing up to provide for me. You afforded us nice things with the number of hours you worked. But you were never there for me as my mom. You could never give me a hundred percent of yourself. I get why now. You were broken. Until I met Leo, I couldn't understand what that meant. Now I do. You said you loved my father and could never move on because there would never be another man who loved you the way he did. I understand that now, too. I'm sorry you lived the last twenty-five years unhappy and hurt. Fix it, Mom. Peter is right in front of you. Eat crow, woman up, and admit all the shitty lies you told. Then get on your knees and beg him to forgive you. I wish you well, but as Leo told you, you aren't welcome in our home if you're going to act like a flaming bitch." I took my first deep breath since I started my tirade and turned to Leo. "Please see my mother and Peter out. I have a headache and need to lie down."

I shut the bedroom door with a gentle click and crawled into bed. What the hell was wrong with that woman? I had never seen her act so crazy before. Sure, she was bossy and she could be a bitch when something crawled up her ass, but this was over the top.

A little while later, Leo came into the room and shut and locked the door. I watched as he took his gun out of the holster and set it on the nightstand. He even locked the door at home if his gun wasn't on him.

"Why didn't you lock the bathroom door in California when you were in the shower? Your gun was off."

"I didn't want the door locked if you needed me," he answered.

He broke his one non-negotiable rule for me. In case I needed him.

In an effort to hide what that meant to me I made a joke. "Sure you did. You were hoping I'd come in and be wowed by your gigantic cock."

Leo threw his head back and laughed long and hard.

Perfection.

"You like my gigantic cock." He laughed.

"Now that I know all the neat tricks it can do, I like it."

"Just like?" he asked, getting into bed next to me.

"I'm pleading the fifth to prevent any further head swelling," I giggled and cuddled into him.

"My head is already swollen," Leo said and slapped my butt.

"I knew you were gonna say that. Lame."

Leo's hand started stroking my hair. "I'm proud of you. You did well today."

"Thanks. I'm sorry she was such a bitch. I don't know what's gotten into her." Leo stopped stroking my hair. "What's wrong?"

"Nothing. I'm sorry I have to leave tonight."

"It's okay. Bella will keep me company," I taunted him.

"Ma's a better choice or MJ. Call MJ if you get bored, he's a stick in the mud. Perfect company for you. Speaking of, I left you all the contact numbers you'll need. All the family's home and cell numbers and the number to the office. It is a direct line to Rena. She's Zane's personal assistant. If there's an emergency, she's the only one who will be able to locate me. You also have the team's cell phone numbers. Though they'll all be with me, except Jasmin and Linc, they'll be around. Don't be surprised if Jasmin comes around under the guise she's checking on you. She's a nosy gossip. I also printed the house listings."

"I'll be fine. I'll ask your mom or Bella to take me to see the houses."

I really didn't want him to go so soon. I was trying not to let my disappointment show.

"Your car is downstairs next to where we parked.

Full disclosure, Jaxon installed a tracking device. Every member of the team has one and please don't take your earring out."

I ignored the fact my car was downstairs, not wanting to know where it had been. The truth was I didn't want to drive that car again.

"You're tracked? Is it in your watch?" I asked, and fiddled with the high-tech looking gadget on his wrist.

"No." Leo stopped for a moment. "We all have chips implanted in our shoulders."

That was a little scary, and I didn't want to examine why he needed a permanent tracking device.

"That's good." Instead, I focused on the benefits of such an implant. If Leo needed help, his team would find him.

"Come here and kiss me. I want to make love to you one more time before I have to go." Leo didn't give me a chance to move. He pulled me on top of him and kissed me breathless.

19

LEO

I looked down at Olivia sleeping in our bed. I fucking loved that – our bed. I really didn't want to leave, but Siles needed to be taken care of. Zane offered for me to stay behind and pull someone up from another team, but I needed to do this. I wanted to be the one that ended Siles' life.

If I didn't leave now, I was afraid I would climb back into bed and love on her again. I double checked all the numbers were left on the counter by her car keys and her new cellphone. I wasn't joking when I threatened to give my baby sister a paddling if she got Olivia into trouble. Olivia thought she was cute and that was the issue. Everyone thought Bella was cute and funny, because she was, right up until she talked you into climbing a water tower to see if you could swim at the top. True story, she did that once while in high school. There were no limits to her hair-brained schemes.

I drove on autopilot to the barn where we were meeting up. With every mile that took me farther from Olivia, my chest tightened a little more. This needed to be done.

When I pulled up to the barn, everyone was already there. No doubt I would get a rash of shit for being late. I rushed through the security protocols and took the stairs to the basement two at a time. Now that I was here, I was eager to get this op started.

"Loverboy finally decided to show up," Jaxon started.

There was no use in stopping it. I leaned against the door and settled in for their ball breaking session. Hell, if I were them, I'd do it, too.

"We were getting ready to call 9-1-1. Thought maybe you had a heart attack. Death by fucking," Colin was the next to chime in.

"I wouldn't be mad if you named your firstborn after me," Garrett said.

Yeah, that wasn't going to happen.

"So, did you untie her before you left?" Eric asked.

I wasn't touching that. I hadn't even talked to Olivia about my adoration for bondage. That was for another day.

"When's the wedding?" Z asked, his face deadly

serious. Unlike the rest of the guys in the room who wanted to bust chops, Zane was asking a real question.

"As soon as we get back and I can buy her a ring," I answered.

"Saw that coming," he mumbled.

"Saw what?" I readied myself for his answer.

"I mean, I saw it the second I climbed into the helicopter and she was on your lap. You looked like you were holding the most precious thing in the world. Before we took off on our drive across country and I was explaining how things worked, you looked like you wanted to take my head off. And what really gave you away was while we were in California, you *did* take my head off and you threatened to take off with the girl."

"Your plan was to trade my woman for information," I reminded him.

"The fuck I was. And if you'd been thinking clearly you would've known I would never trade a human asset for information. I left the fucking agency because they pull that kind of bullshit. I do not trade lives. You have to know it pisses me right the fuck off you'd think that of me."

Fuck. He was right.

"I'm sorry. You're right. I know you better than that," I admitted.

"Good. Let's get hunting, boys. We have a scumbag to dispose of," Zane said.

"Roger that," I answered and moved from in front of the door.

"Happy for you, Panther," Z said as he passed, the smile on his face not reaching his eyes. It was the same smile he gave when he looked at Jasmin and Linc. It was a look of longing.

Iceland was cold as fuck.

I hated the cold and snow. You'd think after all the time I spent over in the Sandbox I'd welcome the cold.

Negative.

I'd take the heat any day. The walk from where the helicopter landed was only a few hundred yards from where the prison Siles was being held, but I was still freezing my balls off.

"Comm check one," came over my earpiece.

"Copy oversight one," I responded.

I heard the other guys answer in turn.

We were fully kitted out, not wanting the prison guards to see our faces. They knew we were coming, they knew to get out of our way, but we still wouldn't show our faces.

"Panther. You're clear to enter. Switching you to comm two. Viper to follow at your six o'clock. Over."

"Roger that," I replied.

Zane gave me point on this op, and he took my

back. He knew I wanted to be the one to end Siles. Unfortunately, there was no other option. This wasn't about revenge; it was about preventing a cartel war in Bolivia that would, in the end, kill thousands of innocent people. The Bolivian government would ask for US aid, and service men and women would be sent in to protect drug territories. We were being proactive and stopping the bloodshed before it happened.

When we entered Siles' cell, he jumped off his cot and put his hands in the air.

"This isn't a stick-up motherfucker. Sit down."

"Sorry, mister, habit. Sorry," he stammered.

"Cut the shit, asshole," Zane shut the door behind us. "Overwatch, we have tango one," Z reported.

"We had a chat with your friend Gomez," Z cut to the chase.

"Please don't take me back, he'll kill me. I gave everything to the Americans. Please, everything I know."

This motherfucker.

"You're caught. Cut the shit and be a man. You were double-crossed on your double-cross, dumbass," Z told him. Siles continued to stare at Zane. "Let me break it down for you in the simplest of terms. Your plan was to have the Americans take out Gomez. You needed bait. A reason for the Americans to want to kill him. What better way than to take the child of a government official? Good plan by the way. I gotta tell you, we were a cunt hair from taking out Gomez for you. Where you got fucked was the second double-cross. That's where a member of your team that was holding Olivia recorded your conversations." Z stopped, and recognition hit Siles. "I see you're understanding now. Those recordings were sent to Gomez. He helpfully provided us with a copy. The AG isn't really happy he helped the man who kidnapped and tortured his daughter."

"What do you want?" Siles asked, the bullshit innocent act dropped.

"Nothing. You have nothing we want. We're here to simply take out the trash," I told him.

"You have a traitor."

Zane rolled his eyes. "Ya think, fucker? We gathered that all on our own. There is not a damn thing you can tell us that we don't already know."

"I can tell you who," Siles said.

"No, you can't. You don't know his name because if you did, you'd already be dead," Z explained.

"It's not a man. It's a woman. I can help you find her. I know her voice." Siles was still trying to save his life.

Holy shit, a woman? There was normally only about twenty percent truth in what a person told you when they were begging for their life. It was completely natural to start making up more information than you really knew in an effort to save yourself.

"Gomez sends his regards. See you in hell." I didn't

give him a chance to answer as my gloved finger followed the trigger guard down, and in one even pull, I squeezed the trigger.

The crack of the bullet sliced through the room, the suppressor only quieting the sonic shockwave. Siles' body slumped to the side. Zane walked over to his body and checked his pulse.

"Extortion three-one on the move," I called in our ride home. "LZ one for pickup."

Zane and I made our way back to the extraction point. Jaxon, Colin, and Eric all stood in front of the helicopter watching our six should anyone try and come out of the prison.

We all piled into the helicopter. "Go," Z instructed the pilot.

Once we were airborne, my body relaxed a little. I was one step closer to getting back to Olivia. I rested my head against the window and enjoyed the vibration of the helicopter.

Seven hours later we were back in DC. Zane called ahead and told Tom we needed a face-to-face. By the time we got to the White House, the situation room had been cleared and ready for our use.

Zane knocked twice on the door and swiped his temporary White House badge.

"Crash code of the day?" a voice said over the intercom.

"Tanker One," Zane answered.

"Color of the day?"

"Red." Zane rolled his eyes.

That about summed it up. The White House protocols were almost as annoying as Zane's need for twenty security checkpoints before you could enter the office.

"Confirmed."

The lock clicked, and Zane pushed open the door. The President sat at the conference table, suit jacket off and his tie loose around his neck.

"Welcome back," Tom greeted.

He looked like shit, like the weight of the world was on his shoulders. I guess being the President, it was.

"Are we secure?" Zane inquired.

"Completely," Tom confirmed.

"We paid a visit to our friend. My balls are still defrosting by the way. He gave us an interesting piece of information. He seemed to think that his contact was a woman. We haven't vetted this intel. But I did want you to know," Zane explained.

"A woman? How reliable do you think this is?" Tom asked.

"I think there's a strong possibility he was telling the truth. It was the way he said it. He was smug like he knew something we didn't and was happy to share. He wasn't running off at the mouth," I interjected.

The whole way back to the states, I was going over what Siles had said and the way he said it. The more I thought about it, the more I believed him.

"I hate to sound like the sexist pig here, but women are easier to turn. It's easy to exploit their emotional side. Women become irrational when a loved one is in danger. If it is a woman, the blackmail started with a close family member. We can also narrow it down to a desk jockey. She's not a field agent and she most likely has access to files," Jaxon explained.

"I don't care if it's a man or a woman. Whoever it is, is a traitor, and I want he or she dealt with accordingly. I'll make sure you have access to whatever you need." Tom stopped and took a drink. "Take a few days, you all need some rest. We'll shelve this for now."

"Copy that. Thank you for your time." Zane handed Tom a file. "For your eyes only. I trust you'll destroy it when you're done."

"One more thing before you go." Tom leveled me with his hard stare. "I heard you've claimed Olivia." Tom put his hand up to stop me when I tried to interrupt. "She's a good girl. I'm happy she has you. She's going to need all the support she can get. Peter told me about your sit down and Pamela's behavior. I need to explain something that could shed some light on her behavior – Pamela has a benign brain tumor. The swelling in her frontal lobe has caused mood swings and aggression. Pamela is normally a mild-mannered woman for the most part. She's currently undergoing treatment to reduce the swelling so she can undergo surgery."

I knew Pamela was ill, Tex had revealed that much, but no one knew the exact details.

"Shit. This is going to kill Olivia. She and Pamela are not on the best of terms. What's the prognosis?" I asked.

"Westinghouse pulled some strings and got her in with the best brain specialist in the country. He's confident he can remove the tumor. But we're talking brain surgery. There are no guarantees."

"I can't keep this from Olivia. She has to know."

I will not start my relationship with my soon-to-be-wife with lies. That was not going to happen.

"I wouldn't expect you to. Pamela should've told her. Right now, it might be better coming from you. I trust you'll tell her when the time is right. Peter is taking care of Pamela. They're working out their issues. What a clusterfuck. I always had my suspicions but never asked. I wish I had. Maybe then both of them wouldn't have spent the last twenty-five years in misery."

"How well do you know Peter Newton? Pamela eluded to him cheating on her while she was away," I asked.

I tried to remember as much of the conversation in the basement when Pamela and Peter came to see Olivia, but the truth was my attention was on Olivia and not Pamela's drama. Olivia looked so broken and lost lying on the bed afterward, I wanted to scoop her up and take her away from all the confusion.

"Peter did not cheat on Pamela with that bitch, Anna Crofton. Anna set Peter up. They were at a party, Peter had too much to drink, and Anna got into bed with him. Took off both their clothes and made Peter think he'd slept with her. A month later she's pregnant and threatening to expose him if Peter didn't marry her. Peter didn't want to marry Anna, but his father demanded he did, as not to embarrass the family. Peter followed orders because back in the day, no one crossed Thad Newton. Shortly after Peter married Anna, she conveniently had a miscarriage. By that time, Thad wouldn't let Peter dump her lying ass because the Croftons had made large investments and donations to Newton businesses. He was stuck with the wench until she died. And I hate to speak ill of the dead, but that woman was a nasty piece of work, and Peter sucked it up. Miserable every day of his life with her. He never stopped loving Pamela."

I didn't know Peter well, but I felt sorry for him. I hoped now that the truth was out they could find a way back to each other. That was, if Pamela pulled through her treatment. I prayed to God she did. This was going to kill my sweet girl.

"That has to be the most fucked up story I've heard," Z said.

"Indeed. You boys get on home." Tom dismissed us.

I rushed through my SITREP while Zane drove back to Maryland. I normally went back to the office to file my reports. But then I'd never had anyone waiting for me to come home before. I sent my report to Garrett and closed my laptop.

Almost home.

EPILOGUE

Leo

It has taken a few months, but I finally did it. I knocked my woman up and got my ring on her finger. Pamela and Ma were so excited they were filling our house with so much baby shit I couldn't find a place to sit.

Once I had all the facts about Pamela's brain tumor, I took Olivia over to Ma's and sat her down with her family surrounding her and laid it out for her. She reacted the way I knew my girl would – she broke down. Ma, Bella, MJ, and Luca all closed ranks and gave her all the love she needed to get through the following weeks. I had never been prouder of my family.

Once my family was told, Olivia and I visited Pamela in DC. We brought Ma along as reinforcement.

Pamela was combative and aggressive and exploded when we confronted her with all the information. In the end, it was Ma who calmed Pamela. She broke down and told Olivia everything. Since that day, Ma and Pamela have forged a close friendship. Pamela was at most Sunday dinners. Peter, too. Olivia was one of us, and by extension, Pamela and Peter had been welcomed into the fold.

Ma was happy; her family was growing by leaps and bounds.

Peter never left Pamela's side. Her surgery was a success, the recovery is still ongoing and would be for a long time. They were slowly working their way back to each other. Peter had proven to be a good dad and was making up for lost time. He called Olivia every day to check in with her. He supported her when she announced she was following her passion for art and going to design school.

My Olivia was happy. And knocked up!

I glanced at my wife in the chair next to me reading some sort of parenting magazine with a breastfeeding mother on the cover. I couldn't wait for Olivia to grow round with my baby.

"Are you nervous?" she asked me when she caught me staring at her.

"Not at all. I know everything is fine."

"Mrs. Gillonardo we're ready for you," the nurse announced.

Mrs. Gillonardo. Goddamn, I loved the sound of that.

We both stood and followed the nurse to the exam room.

"The doctor will be just a moment."

Olivia got herself situated on the exam table, the white paper crinkled as she tried to get comfortable. There was a knock on the door and relief washed over me when a woman in her mid-fifties walked in. The guys had been tormenting me all week at work about Olivia getting a male doctor. They explained all the ways the doctor would be examining my wife.

After the introductions were made, Dr. Lee told Olivia to lie back and squirted a clear jelly all over her lower abdomen. Olivia squeezed my hand and smiled.

"You ready?" she whispered.

Was I ready? Fuck yeah, I was ready. I wanted to yell to the world just how ready I was. Instead, I settled on nodding my head.

The doctor moved a wand over Olivia's belly and the room filled with a swooshing sound.

The most perfect sound.

"One strong heartbeat," the doctor announced.

Nothing could've prepared me for this moment. The first time hearing my child's heartbeat.

Beautiful.

Olivia

I WAS STUFFED, and Essa was still trying to force feed me more.

"You need to eat, *Figlia*," she said.

"Ma, I've eaten two helpings. I can't eat anymore."

"Essa is right, sweetheart, you have to eat," my mom chimed in.

I rolled my eyes at both of them. I hated when they ganged up on me.

"She's eaten more than the boys. Leave her alone." Bella came to my rescue.

God, I loved that girl. She drove her brothers crazy, and I loved watching them get bent out of shape by her antics.

We had a surprise for everyone. Well, it was actually a surprise for all of us. We secretly had a 4D ultrasound. Our moms were going to freak out they weren't there for it, but we hoped that our surprise would make up for it. We also had DVDs of the ultrasound made for them.

Leo came back to the table carrying a beautiful cake covered in white icing.

"That looks lovely, Leo," my mom said.

Once he placed it on the table, I got up and stood by his side. His arm went around me, and he pulled me close.

Always touching me.

"We have an announcement. Grandmas look under your placemats," Leo told them.

I smiled at both women as they found the envelopes under their placements.

"Go ahead and open them," I instructed.

Both of them gasped.

"Is this?" My mom, overcome with emotion, couldn't finish her sentence when she saw what was inside.

"Our grandbaby?" Essa helpfully finished.

I could only nod through my tears. They both looked so happy seeing their grandchild for the first time. The card had a perfect 4D close-up of the baby's face.

"Essa, look at those chubby little cheeks," my mom cried and waved the card around.

"I just, this is the..." Essa couldn't seem to find the words she was looking for. "Thank you, *Figlia*. Thank you for this beautiful baby."

"We have one more surprise. This one is for all of us. Olivia and I don't even know." I looked up at Leo, a sheen of unshed tears in his eyes.

"Dad, will you cut the cake?" I asked Peter.

Peter stood and walked to me, pulled me from Leo's hold, and hugged me tightly. "Thank you," he whispered.

He passed me back to Leo and proudly walked to the table. Peter cut a slice out of the cake and held it up for the room to see. "We have a granddaughter," Peter announced when he saw the pink tinted cake.

A girl.

Leo is going to have a daughter. Oh, Lord! I hoped the world was prepared for Leo being the father of a girl. I knew I wasn't.

The room exploded into cheers and a whole lot of tears. MJ, Luca, and Bella high-fived each other and argued who was going to spoil their niece the most.

The grandparents bickered over who was going to buy her her first dress.

Me and Leo?

We stood hand in hand and watched as the announcement of our daughter had brought the people we loved most in this world joy.

It was a beautiful thing.

SNEAK PEAK–REDEEMING VIOLET

Jaxon

Zane had been pacing for the last hour, I was contemplating duct taping him to the chair or tossing his ass over the balcony into the water below. I wondered what his fancy neighbors would think when they saw a body falling from the penthouse.

"It's not adding up," Zane told me something I already knew. That was the whole reason for our meeting this evening. "The information is classified, yet the hacks are sloppy. If someone was hacking into top secret information, wouldn't they cover their tracks better?"

"They have covered their tracks. We don't know who the fuck they are. It's as if they wanted someone to know the system had been breached, but not who they are," I mused.

It had been too easy to find where Olivia Cox had been kept. Too easy to trace that someone from Langley had hacked into the White House server. And way too easy to pin it on Timothy Clark. Why would anyone want us to find all the breadcrumbs they were leaving but not their identity?

Zane's phone rang and he pulled it out of his pocket looking at the screen. "Goddamn telemarketers. I'm writing the fucking phone company a letter tomorrow about the do not fucking call registry. I'm on the list. Assholes." Zane angerly swiped his phone stopping the ringing. Before he could repocket his phone it started ringing again. This time he answered placing the call on speaker.

"Hello," he barked. It was hard to suppress the laugh that was bubbling.

"Zane Lewis?" a woman asked.

Zane turned to me and rolled his eyes. "Yes. Who is this?" he asked.

"My name is Violet Myers. I am with the CIA. I believe you've been looking for me?"

"Why would I be looking for you?" he asked and motioned for me to trace the call.

"There is no time for games. There has been a breach and a SEAL platoon is walking into an ambush. They were deployed two hours ago out of San Diego. I'm working on my end to find their exact location. With your resources, I thought it would be faster to work together," Violet replied. "And there is no need to try and trace this call. I have emailed you all my intel and I will give you my cell number before we hang up. I'm actually on my way to you right now. I had to leave Virginia."

"On your way to me?" Zane asked still trying to stall so I could triangulate her location.

"Yes, to your condo. ETA five minutes," she replied.

"The fuck you say?" Zane Lewis had gone from pissed to nuclear.

"Mr. Lewis, I don't think you need me to repeat myself. Do you want to play these games and explain to Caroline why her husband Matthew and his team didn't come home? Or do you want to work together and warn them."

"I swear to Christ woman, if you leaked information that gets them killed I will personally cut your throat and watch your blood spill," Zane yelled.

"And I will gladly stand in front of you while you do. I'm ready to turn myself in and help but I need a favor." Violet had lost the bravado she had at the start of the conversation.

"You have some balls asking me for a favor. What could you possibly want from me?" Zane glanced at me and I turned my laptop in his direction. Sure as shit, the woman was turning down his street headed straight to us.

"I'll tell you when I come up. I'm here now." The

call disconnected and I thought Zane was going to crush his phone.

"Call Tex," Zane yelled over his shoulder as he moved to his bedroom, no doubt to pull out the heavy artillery. Zane can be a scary motherfucker when he was pissed.

Tex picked up on the first ring. "Tex, it's Jaxon. I'm unsecure," I informed him.

"Copy that," he replied, apprehension thick.

"Sorry to bother you. I need confirmation that the Frogs have gone to play in the Sandbox," I asked using the nickname for SEALs and the universal term for the Middle East.

"I'd say that sounds about right," he replied.

"We have a problem. Track them and tell them to hold fast for further intel and possible EXFIL. Possible mission compromise."

"Fuck. Copy." Tex disconnected. There was no one better at tracking. I had faith that we'd have their location within the hour. Hopefully, before the team landed.

Redeeming Violet

ABOUT THE AUTHOR

Riley Edwards is a bestselling multi-genre author, wife, and military mom. Riley was born and raised in Los Angeles but now resides on the east coast with her fantastic husband and children.

Riley writes heart-stopping romance with sexy alpha heroes and even stronger heroines. Riley's favorite genres to write are romantic suspense and military romance.

Riley Edwards Newsletter –
https://www.subscribepage.com/RRsignup
Add Riley Edwards on Goodreads
http://geni.us/goodreadsre

facebook.com/Novelist.Riley.Edwards

OTHER BOOKS BY RILEY EDWARDS

AVAILABLE ON AMAZON

The Red Team

Nightstalker

Protecting Olivia

Redeeming Violet

Recovering Ivy (TBA)

The 707 Freedom Series

Free

Freeing Jasper

Finally Free

Freedom

The Next Generation

All the Pretty Girls

The Gift

The Masters Collection

The Awakening

The Collective

Unbroken 1 & 2 – Season One

Trust – Season Two (Fall of 2018)

More Books in the Special Forces: Operation Alpha World!

Brynne Asher: Blackburn
Denise Agnew: Dangerous to Hold
Shauna Allen: Awakening Aubrey
Shauna Allen: Defending Danielle
Shauna Allen: Rescuing Rebekah
Shauna Allen: Saving Scarlett
Shauna Allen: Saving Grace
Jennifer Becker: Hiding Catherine
Julia Bright: Saving Lorelei
Victoria Bright: Surviving Savage
Victoria Bright: Going Ghost
Victoria Bright: Jostling Joker
Kendra Mei Chailyn: Beast
Kendra Mei Chailyn: Barbie
Kendra Mei Chailyn : Pitbull
Melissa Kay Clarke: Rescuing Annabeth
Melissa Kay Clarke: Safeguarding Miley
Samantha A. Cole: Handling Haven
Samantha A. Cole: Cheating the Devil
Sue Coletta: Hacked
KaLyn Cooper: Rescuing Melina
Liz Crowe: Marking Mariah
Jordan Dane: Redemption for Avery
Jordan Dane: Fiona's Salvation

Riley Edwards: Protecting Olivia
Riley Edwards: Redeeming Violet
Nicole Flockton: Protecting Maria
Nicole Flockton: Guarding Erin
Nicole Flockton: Guarding Suzie
Nicole Flockton: Guarding Brielle
Casey Hagen: Shielding Nebraska
Casey Hagen: Shielding Harlow
Casey Hagen: Shielding Josie
Desiree Holt: Protecting Maddie
Kathy Ivan: Saving Sarah
Kathy Ivan: Saving Savannah
Kathy Ivan: Saving Stephanie
Jesse Jacobson: Protecting Honor
Jesse Jacobson: Fighting for Honor
Jesse Jacobson: Defending Honor
Jesse Jacobson: Summer Breeze
Silver James: Rescue Moon
Silver James: SEAL Moon
Silver James: Assassin's Moon
Becca Jameson: Saving Sofia
Kate Kinsley: Protecting Ava
Heather Long: Securing Arizona
Heather Long: Guarding Gertrude
Heather Long: Protecting Pilar
Heather Long: Covering Coco
Kirsten Lynn: Joining Forces for Jesse

Jen Talty: Burning Kiss
Jen Talty: Burning Skies
Jen Talty: Burning Lies
Megan Vernon: Protecting Us
Megan Vernon: Protecting Earth

As you know, this book included at least one character from Susan Stoker's books. To check out more, see below.

Delta Force Heroes Series

Rescuing Rayne (FREE!)

Rescuing Aimee (novella)

Rescuing Emily

Rescuing Harley

Marrying Emily

Rescuing Kassie

Rescuing Bryn

Rescuing Casey

Rescuing Sadie

Rescuing Wendy

Rescuing Mary (Oct 2018)

Rescuing Macie (April 2019)

Badge of Honor: Texas Heroes Series

Justice for Mackenzie (FREE!)

Justice for Mickie

Justice for Corrie

Justice for Laine (novella)

Shelter for Elizabeth

Justice for Boone

Shelter for Adeline

Shelter for Sophie

Justice for Erin

Justice for Milena
Shelter for Blythe
Justice for Hope (Sept 2018)
Shelter for Quinn (Feb 2019)
Shelter for Koren (June 2019)
Shelter for Penelope (Oct 2019)

SEAL of Protection Series

Protecting Caroline (FREE!)
Protecting Alabama
Protecting Fiona
Marrying Caroline (novella)
Protecting Summer
Protecting Cheyenne
Protecting Jessyka
Protecting Julie (novella)
Protecting Melody
Protecting the Future
Protecting Kiera (novella)
Protecting Dakota

SEAL of Protection: Legacy Series

Securing Caite (Jan 2019)
Securing Sidney (May 2019)
Securing Piper (Sept 2019)
Securing Zoey (TBA)
Securing Avery (TBA)
Securing Kalee (TBA)

New York Times, *USA Today* and *Wall Street Journal* Bestselling Author Susan Stoker has a heart as big as the state of Texas where she lives, but this all American girl has also spent the last fourteen years living in Missouri, California, Colorado, and Indiana. She's married to a retired Army man who now gets to follow *her* around the country.

She debuted her first series in 2014 and quickly followed that up with the SEAL of Protection Series, which solidified her love of writing and creating stories readers can get lost in.

If you enjoyed this book, or any book, please consider leaving a review. It's appreciated by authors more than you'll know.

www.stokeraces.com
www.AcesPress.com
susan@stokeraces.com

37415312R10143

Printed in Poland
by Amazon Fulfillment
Poland Sp. z o.o., Wrocław